THE LINES

The Iowa Review Series in Fiction

Harilaos Stecopoulos, series editor

THE LINES

A Novel

ANTHONY VARALLO

UNIVERSITY OF IOWA PRESS | IOWA CITY

University of Iowa Press, Iowa City 52242

Copyright © 2019 by Anthony Varallo

www.uipress.uiowa.edu

Printed in the United States of America

No part of this book may be reproduced or used in any form or by any means without permission in writing from the publisher. All reasonable steps have been taken to contact copyright holders of material used in this book. The publisher would be pleased to make suitable arrangements with any whom it has not been possible to reach.

Printed on acid-free paper

Library of Congress Cataloging-in-Publication Data

Names: Varallo, Anthony, 1970– author.

Title: The lines : a novel / Anthony Varallo.

Description: Iowa City, IA : University of Iowa Press, [2019] | Series: The Iowa Review series in fiction |

Identifiers: LCCN 2019002004 (print) | LCCN 2019005069 (ebook) | ISBN 978-1-60938-666-5 (ebook) | ISBN 978-1-60938-665-8 (pbk. : alk. paper)

Subjects: LCSH: Dysfunctional families.

Classification: LCC PS3622.A725 (ebook) | LCC PS3622.A725 L56 2019 (print) | DDC 813/.6—dc23

LC record available at https://lccn.loc.gov/2019002004

For my mother, my father,
and my sister, Marie

THE LINES

ONE

THE PARENTS TELL the children to come upstairs. They have something to tell them, they say. The children are in the basement, where they have been playing Smash Up Derby, a game of their own invention, a game they have twice already been cautioned not to play. In Smash Up Derby, one child sits at one end of the basement while the other child—there are two of them, brother and sister, the boy and the girl—sits at the other end, cross-legged, clutching a toy car. "Ready?" the girl asks, and the boy responds, "Ready." They count to three and send the cars careening into one another, a head-on collision. "Smash Up Derby!" the boy shouts, even though the girl has told him not to do that. The boy is seven years old and has no idea about anything. The girl turns ten next month and has some things figured out.

When the parents call for them, the children give each other a look. They know what is about to happen: they will be summoned upstairs and given a lecture about playing Smash Up Derby. They will be in trouble. They will be instructed to clean up their cars and head straight to their rooms. They will be punished. The children ascend the stairs, the certainty of what is to follow so real, so obvious, so beyond debate that, for years afterward, it is the thing the boy remembers more than anything else about this evening, the feeling of climbing the basement stairs, his sister ahead of him, the basement door open wide, his parents waiting for them, a punishment on the way, in this house where his mother and father preside, watchful, alert, and wise to everything the children do.

Upstairs, the children find their parents sitting on the family room sofa. Apart. Their father is leaning forward, rubbing his hands together, his tie still hanging loosely from his neck. Their mother sits at the opposite end of the sofa, her face strangely red, raw looking. The children thought their parents were watching TV, but the TV is off. Why is the TV off? The girl has been wording her apology the entire way up the basement stairs, but before she can speak, the mother says, "Your father has something to tell you two." And then she bursts into tears. Big, wracking sobs that signal the two of them are really in trouble this time.

But when the father speaks, he begins to cry too, and his words fail to match the words the boy expects the father to use. Instead of saying, "We have told you time and time again not to play that game," the father says, "Your mother and I have decided to separate," and instead of saying, "And yet you continue to play that game," the father says, "I've rented an apartment nearby," and when his father should be saying, "We're taking away your toys for the next week," he instead says, "I know how hard this is for you to understand," and in place of "You may now go to your rooms," comes "But your mother and I have decided that this is the best thing for us," while "We're both very disappointed in you" has been commandeered by his father putting his head in his hands.

It is a miracle, the boy thinks. They will not be punished after all. How often do the things we fear never come to pass. So true! The boy feels giddy, alive, afloat with this new knowledge, and turns to his sister to see if she's caught on to it as well, but she only throws her arms around her father and says, "Daddy, oh Daddy, no."

————

HIS LAST FEW weeks in the house, the father sleeps in the guest bedroom. The bedroom is the one the children's grandmother uses when she visits from Florida, injecting the house with crossword puzzles, cigarettes, and late-night television—she can only fall asleep to Johnny Carson. Now, the guest room TV stares blankly at the boy as he sits on the bed next to his father. It is morning, and the boy must get to school, three tedious weeks left until summer vacation, but the father has asked him to come sit next to him while he gets ready for work. So the boy complies. Downstairs, his sister tarries in the bathroom, brushing her never-long-enough hair into infinity.

"Big day at school today?" the father asks.

"Nah," the boy says.

"What's on the agenda?"

The boy shrugs, says he doesn't know.

"Tests?"

"No."

"Quizzes?"

The boy shakes his head.

"Show and tell?"

"Nah."

"Field trip?"

The boy gives his father a look that says, *I know you are just kidding about the field trip,* and the father returns one that wishes to say, *Yes, but kidding around is what I do best, right?* The boy thinks the father is about to make another joke, but lately the world keeps wishing the boy to know he has little idea about anything at all. His father pulls him close, leaving just enough room for the boy to glimpse their reflection in the TV screen, dull as a pigeon's eye.

———

THE CHILDREN's grandmother calls them on the phone. Gumma, the children call her, to distinguish her from their other grandmother, Grandmom, who lives nearby and who does not drink margaritas late into the evening, as Gumma does. Gumma lives

3

in Florida in a house a mile from the beach, the house fitted out with a refrigerator that can be accessed from the outside (an outside refrigerator! thrilling to the boy, the one time they vacationed there, reaching in and grabbing another cold Dr. Pepper on the sly). Gumma owns a golf cart she once permitted the girl to drive, the children laughing, saying, *Floor it!* as Gumma sat beside them, sipping a margarita from a plastic tumbler. One time, she tried to teach the children how to make margaritas for her, but the parents said no. When the parents were out of earshot, Gumma whispered, "Next time."

But Gumma rarely calls the children on the phone. Why is Gumma calling them on the phone? Gumma's voice sounds strange, off, her mouth harboring ice, which makes faint crunching noises when she says, "I'm calling to check up on you two."

"Oh," the girl says.

"Two sweet little children without their daddy in the house."

"Well," the girl says.

"Let's have some girl talk just between us," Gumma says. "The fact is men will be after you now. They'll sense your father is gone." The girl can hear Gumma crunching a prodigious ice cube. "But like I said, that's just between us, OK?"

"OK," the girl says, and listens as Gumma describes some other things she needs to be aware of, things the girl would rather not be aware of, thank you very much, so she hands the phone to her brother, who says "Gumma?" three times before Gumma realizes it's him.

"You, young man, you've got to protect your sister and mother," she tells him. "Leave some of your father's old stuff around the house. Clothes. Shoes. Boots are good. Make strangers think he's still around."

After the call, the children brush their teeth without speaking to one another.

———

THE CHILDREN attend the same school. Each morning they wait at the end of their neighborhood, backpacks tossed into the dewy grass, until a bus appears and swallows them whole. The ride to school: a filmstrip of fields, neighborhoods, and wooded rural roads framed by double-hung windows that eventually yields to the highway, where other buses show other children staring back at them. Leaving the bus, a minor thrill, the bus stairs higher than the curb, requiring a jump the boy always imagines as crossing from one rooftop to another. At the school entrance, the children part ways, off to different classrooms.

The morning announcements arrive courtesy of speakers mounted above the chalkboard, where an American flag flies. The first bell sends the girl from her homeroom to the art room, her still life incomplete, its first brushstrokes, the girl realizes, completed when her parents were still together. Should she leave the painting unfinished? The art room sink shelters a dozen plastic cups crammed with paintbrushes, their bristles wetly caked with paint. The girl washes her brushes and adds them to the others. She knows her still life is terrible, despite her teacher's enthusiasm. The grapes look like marbles. A halved apple rests flatly on a rotting banana, each fruit stranded in a warring perspective. For the rest of the day, the girl's hands exude the smell of paint.

The boy spends his morning in homeroom. Today, the class has reading time, during which they must read an assigned book, a sop to those students who, unlike the boy, never do the assigned reading at home. So the boy reads ahead of the assigned chapters, but without quite paying attention. He can do that sometimes, read without really reading, even though his eyes move across the page, and he's aware of one sentence yielding to the next. Especially with sentences that have talking in them, like when Frank says to Joe, "Look out!" and Joe says, "There he goes! Quick, let's get him!" Reading those sentences is like reading nothing at all.

———

SOMETIMES THE girl can't stand her brother. She really can't. Like the way he's always picking his nose and then acting like he wasn't picking his nose, when he was very clearly and beyond any reasonable doubt picking his nose.

"That's disgusting," the girl says.

"What?" the boy says.

"Picking your nose."

"I wasn't," the boy says, even though he's still doing it. Doesn't even know how to cover his tracks.

"Don't wipe your hands on the sofa."

"I'm not," the boy says. But he is.

"That's so disgusting," the girl says.

The boy shrugs. He doesn't know the littlest thing. Doesn't know how foolish he looks when he hops around the house with some dumb idea asserting itself inside his head, his arms wild, loose. The way everyone can see him doing that, his mother, father, and sister, all aware of what he's doing, while he's oblivious.

The poor slob, the girl thinks. What will become of him now?

———

HERE'S A surprise for the children: spring weather continues to be spring weather, despite everything. Despite everything, the mother keeps the children's bedroom windows open at night, the air so cool the girl must keep the afghan her aunt knitted for her — that's the word they use for it, *afghan*, which, the girl thinks, must mean a blanket that is more holes than yarn — at the foot of her bed. Mornings, the afghan has fallen to the floor; the girl reaches for it and finds sleep again.

Afternoons, the sun sends long rectangles of light across the lunchroom floor. Recess wants them to know one thing and one thing only: it is hot outside. Even the slim column of shade beneath the sliding board offers little comfort. Cut grass sticks to shoes.

Spring showers are a respite, a relief. Trees turn their leaves up, showing their pale undersides, as tender as the boy's underarms, which will not redden until summer, when his father takes the children swimming at his apartment complex's pool, shaped like a kidney and rimmed with women reclining on lounge chairs, their sunglasses making it impossible to tell whether they're sleeping or watching you ride your father's shoulders for the third time that afternoon.

The day after it rains, worms appear on the driveway.

"Leave them alone," the boy's sister tells him, when he's about to prod one with a stick. "What did they ever do to you?"

Yet another question the boy has no answer for.

———

THE WORLD IS running out of gas, it's true. Everybody knows. America is a nation on empty. Even the president has no idea what to do. When the boy accompanies his mother to the gas station near their neighborhood, the one at the intersection, the one where, in great barrels topped with glass lids, fat pickles float in liquid the color of grass and defy the boy's attempts to grab them with tongs, he sees cars waiting in lines that stretch out onto the highway. His mother sighs. Doesn't want to wait but can't afford not to wait either. So wait in line they must, windows down, on this oppressive afternoon with the air redolent of exhaust. In every car, as far as the boy can see, drivers and passengers and children with their arms slung loosely outside open windows, waiting for a breeze that never comes.

A sign at the station's weedy entrance: MAKE A BIG SPLASH TRY CARPOOLING NEXT TIME.

———

ON SUNDAYS, the children attend mass with their mother. There is nothing more boring than mass. It is incredible how boring mass is, and still they keep going, the three of them, always late, always having to say, *Sorry, excuse us*, as they find an open seat in the middle of a pew. The girl looks for cute boys while pretending to read the hymnal. Sometimes the girl senses boys looking at her in church, curious, appraising, especially during communion, when she must walk reverently to the communion rail, kneel, receive the host—she cannot bear the sight of the priest's wristwatch, up close, visible just beneath his sleeve—and return to her seat again. The girl feels the boys' eyes on her. There's a power in not looking back at them, the girl realizes; you can win as easily by not doing something as doing something. She's catching on to things like that now. The girl swallows the host.

The boy has recently been forbidden to bring his action figures to church and now must suffer through the prayers of intercession without Spiderman and Batman to suffer along with him, their faces determinedly set on fighting crime, indifferent to the congregation's *Lord, hear our prayer*. The boy prays for peace, for health, for the repose of the soul of . . . all without recognition. He kneels when it is time to kneel. Rises when everyone else rises. Incense, shaken from burners attached to short chains, seems the fragrance of boredom itself.

This morning, their mother drives them to the early mass, all older women in hats and grandfather-types extending baskets on long poles. It is the girl's job to drop a dollar bill into the basket, but today the mother has forgotten her money, so the girl lets the basket pass, her face warm with embarrassment. After mass, they drive home without stopping to get donuts and a newspaper at the gas station, the way they usually do. They cruise past the intersection as if the gas station isn't even there. Has their mother forgotten how much they all like powdered donuts and the newspaper, the mother with her entertainment section and weekly ads, the children dividing the comics in two, arguing, sometimes, over who will get *Peanuts* first?

Home, the mother says she's going to take a short nap. She lies down on the family room sofa and instructs the children to wake her in fifteen minutes. "Set the oven timer," she says, and the girl sets the oven timer. But fifteen minutes later, when the timer sounds, their mother does not rise. Instead, she turns from her position on the sofa and finds another position, her eyes closed. The children watch, afraid to wake her. What should they do?

After a while, the girl says, "Mom? Do you want to wake up?"

She's still wearing her church clothes, wrinkled now, most likely.

"Mom?"

Their mother opens her eyes. Sits up, startled, and says, "We're late for mass!"

The children say, "No, Mom. We already went to mass, remember?"

The mother looks at them, disbelievingly. "We did?"

"Yeah," the girl says.

"Oh," the mother says. She regards her clothes now, straightens the hem of her skirt. How pretty she still is, the girl thinks. "I don't remember," the mother says, and then smiles, experimentally. "Isn't that funny?"

"Yeah," the children say. Is it funny? The children are not sure.

"What happened at mass?"

"Not much," the boy says.

"The same old," the girl says.

"The same old," the mother says.

The girl says, "We forgot our dollar."

"Oh," the mother says. "For the collection." But then she lies back down on the sofa and eventually falls asleep again.

———

ONE AFTERNOON, the father says to the children, "Come upstairs." The children are watching TV while their father packs things into boxes. Their mother is wherever their mother is: she has gotten good at disappearing whenever their father is back in the house—but then again, everything is disappearing in this house. See the corner where the father's dresser used to stand, how bright the carpet beneath it, how clean, untouched, and preserved. How little unhappiness it was ever called to witness.

"This is my old savings bank," the father says, once the children have arrived in the guest room. The bank is shaped like a cash register, with a coin slot, a lever, a deposit display, and a door that opens at the bottom. "I got this when I was six years old," the father says. "It's probably my oldest material possession." The children nod, say wow, how cool, but they know the father is mostly talking to himself. Plus, they've also heard this story before and have played with the bank a dozen times, a disappointing toy. Drop a coin inside and the bank keeps it. A cruel trick. But they must listen to their father, for whom this bank means something. Parents, the children think; it's all a matter of giving them a little encouragement.

"Now, I've already put two dollars in here so that you'll have a head start, but I want you two to keep saving up your change until you reach ten dollars, because when you reach ten dollars," here, the father gives them a hopeful, expectant look, one the children must return in kind, "see this little door at the bottom? Well, when you reach ten dollars, this little door finally opens up and you can get all the money you've saved." He hands the bank to the girl. "You two will have to tell me how much you're saving, OK?"

The children tell him OK.

"I'll want a full report."

But only a week after the father moves out, the children have forgotten about the bank. Somehow it has ended up in the boy's room, beneath his desk, there among his least loved toys, where it marks time beside a stuffed frog the boy won in a school raffle and a souvenir tomahawk from a class field trip he can't even remember now aside from the gift shop, fitted out with bright arrows, glittering weapons, and painted tom-toms. Once, the boy finds a dime in the laundry room—preternaturally shiny; it must have been run through the wash—and remembers about the bank. He places the dime in the slot, pulls the lever, and watches the bank display change from two dollars to two dollars and ten cents. Immediately, he feels regret. Misses the dime like something gone. Why didn't he just keep it?

———

HERE'S SOMETHING terrible and horrible the boy must not think about if he ever wants to fall asleep at night the way he is supposed to: last year, two teenagers were killed in a car accident just outside the boy's neighborhood. Their car hit a tree on the little twisty road whose name the boy has never bothered to learn. The one where, if you follow the wooden fence that borders the soccer fields with your eyes sort of half-squinting and your head turned just slightly so, it makes it look like the fence is moving but you aren't. The way the rails get blurry and strange. An illusion of some kind the boy isn't curious enough to solve.

But here's something the boy wonders about, on those nights

when he is trying to fall asleep and not think about the teenagers who died: were they watching the fence just before they hit the tree?

———

THE CHILDREN have a pet cat. An outdoor cat, they explain to visitors, to justify those long expanses of time when the cat is no-where to be found. Last summer, for example, or this April. The cat's fur is mottled brown and gray. The cat has white paws, the thing everyone always marvels about. An expired flea collar hangs loosely from the cat's neck.

A story about the cat: when the children's parents were first dating—the children cannot quite imagine this era somehow, ter-rible to think of time that didn't include them—the mother told the father she always wanted to have a cat. Wasn't allowed to have one as a kid, didn't know if she could afford one now. Probably would have to wait until later, she reasoned. Until she was a re-sponsible adult, ha. But why would anyone wait for a thing like that? their crafty father said, and, the *very next day*, produced from the folds of his winter jacket the family-cat-to be, a surprise kitten. The mother fed the kitten milk from a rinsed lid. The kitten drank so fast! His tongue nudging the lid across the kitchen floor.

Now, a week before the father moves into his apartment, the parents and children are sharing a silent meal on the back patio when the cat materializes from the backyard bushes.

"Look," the girl whispers. "It's the cat."

"Kitty-kitty!" the boy calls.

"Shh," the girl admonishes. "You'll scare him away again."

"I'll grab him," the father says, but the moment he stands from the table the cat darts back into the bushes.

THE GIRL TAKES piano lessons at home. Her piano teacher is a girl from the neighborhood—a *college girl*, the girl has heard her mother say to others, to family—although the piano teacher wears cutoffs, halter tops, and sandals, and talks like a teenager: her sentences do a funny thing where they go up like she's asking a question even when she's not asking a question. I think you'll really like these exercises? I could circle all the tempo changes? Today's lesson is a dumbed-down version of Bach's "Little Fugue" the girl hasn't even practiced, aside from this morning, when she couldn't get the triplets to work out right. The girl can't stand triplets. Triplets have been giving her grief for the past two lessons, but the piano teacher has told the girl not to worry, she'll get them soon, just keep practicing. But the girl does not practice, and each week gets stuck on the same things, and each week hears the piano teacher's encouragement, on and on. Maybe music lessons are like that everywhere, the girl thinks: students promise to practice, neglect practice, promise again, neglect again, while the teacher keeps showing up at three-thirty each Wednesday, acting as if the fun has just begun.

Today, the piano teacher arrives a few minutes late. Sorry, she says. She had to do some laundry and lost track of the time and then she couldn't find her assignment book, which, it turns out, she'd left right by the door so she wouldn't forget it. Ha! Lately, it seems like everything is like that? Like, last week? She was looking everywhere for her biology textbook, and the whole time it was in her backpack, right where it was supposed to be? Next time, she'll just look where something is supposed to be right from the start? Wouldn't that be something? As the piano teacher speaks, the girl realizes that the teacher is uncomfortable now, nervous to be in this house where parents are splitting up, as she surely must know. To make the piano teacher feel at ease, the girl laughs and says she does things like that all the time too. Gives her a few examples. Makes up a few because making a few up is simple. The piano teacher laughs, relieved. This is still a house where the girl can laugh. The girl watches the piano teacher and thinks, Adults, what an easy crowd.

The girl plays the "Little Fugue." One measure yields to the next. And then another measure yields yet again to another. She makes it to the tenth measure without making a serious mistake. For the first time, the girl grasps the truth about triplets: triplets are as much about the spaces between the notes as the notes themselves. Ignore those spaces and you're lost. Obey the spaces. The girl plays the piece to the end, only stopping once. When she finishes, she turns to her teacher to see if she's surprised too but is disappointed to see the teacher with her hands to her mouth, crying.

"I knew you could do it!" she says. "Oh, I'm so proud of you!" The piano teacher gives the girl a hug, her clothes reeking of patchouli.

"Thanks," the girl says, but really, if there's anything less in the world the girl wants to see right now than a crying adult, she doesn't know what it is.

———

FIRST IMPRESSIONS of the father's new apartment: the soda machines at the end of each hallway, glowing wanly in the afternoon. The pool! From the balcony, you can almost see the mall where the arcade is. The lock, chain, and padlock on the front door. The peephole. A kitchen so narrow you have to wait for someone to leave before you can open the refrigerator door. The pool! Using all the old plates and silverware from when they were toddlers. The cereal bowls with the sunflower design. The elevator. Greeting people in the hallway. The way everything smells like chlorine.

Hearing the neighbor's TV. The shower that turns the water hot when you turn the knob to COLD and turns the water cold when you turn it to HOT. Learning the apartment number.

MORNINGS, the mother must drive past the children on the way to work. The children wait for their bus with a group of other kids. The children seem embarrassed by her in the presence of others, the mother can tell. They look away. Perhaps the children resent her presence among these classmates, whose families are presumably happier, thriving, or at least not dividing kitchenware into cardboard boxes and sealing the boxes with a screech of packing tape. The children might even hate her now. They might. That's something the mother could never imagine them feeling before, but separation has taken whatever she could never imagine before and said, That's all you got? The mother slows the car, considers giving the horn a quick tap, decides not to. Pulls away.

TWO

RAIN. It rains nearly every other day now. The lawn grows high. Their father offers to cut it, but the mother says no. She'll do it. But she doesn't do it; the grass gets so tall that, a week later, the boy's sneakers can disappear into it. Another disappearing act, to go along with his father's car, no longer parked in the garage, no longer requiring the boy to navigate his way around it when retrieving his bicycle. The space where the car used to be, a constellation of oil stains.

The weather is hot enough for them to open the windows, but not hot enough yet to require air conditioning, their mother says. The boy sleeps with a fan at the foot of his bed. The fan turns from side to side, blows air onto him, but also onto nothing, which depresses the boy. The fan has three speeds, but the boy always sets the fan to HIGH. What good is LOW?

Whenever a sudden thunderstorm appears, the mother says, "Close the windows!" which is the girl's signal to say, "I'll get upstairs!" and then ascend the stairs as fast as she can until she reaches the guest bedroom, where both windows are open, the screens newly studded with raindrops, the rain coming down now, the wind picking up. The girl could easily close both windows in an instant, but she doesn't. She hesitates, just for a moment, and permits the rain to freckle the windowsill, this rain that cares nothing for her or their house or their carpets or their family or their problems or anything about them really. Then the girl closes the windows.

"There," she says, as if something has been settled at last.

ON WEEKENDS the children stay with their father. He picks them up on Friday and takes them to dinner and, later, a movie. The children's mother packs a suitcase for each of them, too large really, but the children refuse to share, as they used to when they were younger. The girl needs her outfits, which have grown up lately, requiring just this skirt, just this top, or just this pair of shoes. The boy, to keep pace, packs books, a sketchpad, and stuffed animals. He is nearly too old for stuffed animals, but the weekend visits — and the suitcase — give him a license to bring them along, their permanent smiles and goofy grins following him to the apartment bedroom, where the boy neglects to place them on his pillows as he does at home.

But — restaurants! The children have never been to so many restaurants. The father takes them to restaurants where men and women congregate around a bar ceilinged with flipped wine-glasses, and a pretty hostess, her hair tied back into a ponytail, invites them to follow her through a dark dining area to a table wearing a cloth the boy must be careful not to tug as he did last weekend, tipping a water glass onto its side.

The waitress hands them each a menu and describes the specials. The girl watches her father when the waitress describes the specials: he is an excellent audience, says, That sounds good, or Aha, or Delicious, or nods his head and looks at the children, as if to say, These specials are tempting and inviting to all of us, aren't they? The children nod. The waitress asks them what they would like. The girl orders linguini off the adult menu, while her brother sticks to the children's burger, which arrives with an embarrassing clown hat impaled on its bun.

Dinner conversation: which movie should they see? What are their choices? The father asks the waitress for a newspaper; the waitress complies, brings the entertainment section of the local paper, the movie listings on the last page, along with the crossword, the comics. The father limits their choices to G-rated films, but they always end up seeing something PG anyway. Tonight, they choose an animated film, long on singing, short on story, but the children lie and say they liked it, later, when the father holds the theater door for them. Outside, it is night. The children rarely stay up this late. The boy falls asleep in the car.

"Guess we should have picked an earlier movie," the father says. "Sorry."

The girl tells him it's OK; they sleep in on the weekends now. The girl says she can make cereal and toast for herself and her brother in the morning too, no problem. She can even make eggs, even if all she knows how to do is scrambled. They can do things by themselves now.

"I didn't know you could make scrambled eggs," the father says.

The girl reminds her father that he was the one who showed her how.

The father says, "I did?"

"Use the big blue bowl. Crack the eggs on the side. Make sure no eggshell falls in. Add a little cheese."

"That's right," the father says. He turns a smile on her and says, "That's absolutely right," but whether the smile is to convey his pleasure in teaching her something useful or to hide his embarrassment for forgetting it altogether, the girl cannot say.

———

AS SOON AS the children are out of school, the mother starts taking classes two nights a week, requiring a babysitter, or worse, an evening in the care of their grandparents, sometimes at the grandparents' home, nearly an hour away. The children beg their mother to let them stay home alone. Please, we're old enough now, they say, but the mother isn't convinced.

"If something happens, we can call a neighbor," the children say.

"Which neighbor?" the mother asks.

The children list names, options, possibilities.

"So you would call them and say, 'Help, our kitchen is on fire? What should we do?'"

The children say no; they would call the fire department if the kitchen caught on fire.

Their mother says, "What would you do that sets the kitchen on fire?"

But the mother must leave them alone sometimes. No other choice. That they never talk about it is the mother's signal that they are never to talk about it. "I've left two sandwiches for you in the fridge," she says. "You can stay up to eight-thirty, but I want you in bed by eight-fifteen." But at eight-fifteen, the boy cannot bring himself to put himself to bed. Might as well ask him to cut his own hair or trim his toenails, two things the boy would point out that he needs taken care of, by the way, if he weren't so busy trying to fall asleep with his bedroom light on, his rosary clutched between his doubting fingers, in the event that a vampire might appear. At eight-twenty, his sister yells at him to turn the light off. She's down the hall in her room, her light on too.

"I can't help it," the boy says.

"If you don't turn off that light, I'm going to smash it," the girl says, an idle threat if there ever was one, but enough to make the boy cry, the little baby.

"I can't help it!"

"Turn it off," the girl says.

"I can't," the boy says, pulls the covers over his head, and repeats the words often enough that they become a kind of abject prayer, *I can't, I can't, I can't*, until he is able to fall asleep.

——————

THE MOTHER must study for her classes. She buys expensive textbooks (she complains about the price; the children overhear her talking to friends on the phone, saying, "Thirty-six dollars for a book I'm never going to use again. And it's not even a nice book. It's ugly! Thirty-six dollars for an ugly book I'm never going to use again!") and highlights them with a thrilling, thick yellow marker that glistens whenever the mother drags its tip through a sentence, *the eight fundamental aspects of the accounting cycle*, leaving a faint whiff of ink that vanishes in an instant. Nights, the mother stays up late, the expensive, ugly books spread across the kitchen table, open to reveal whole pages inked in yellow. Mornings, the children must move the books aside to eat their cereal. After a while, they give up on the kitchen table altogether; they eat breakfast in the family room, as they do lunch and dinner.

——————

SOME NIGHTS, the children have a babysitter. The babysitter is in high school. The babysitter is a boy, a rarity for babysitters, at least in the children's fairly limited experience of the species. The babysitter drives a Pontiac Firebird, a car he talks about frequently and with great feeling. The thing about the babysitter's Pontiac Firebird, the babysitter would like the children to know, is how cool it feels to be behind the wheel, driving. That's about the coolest thing in the world. You know? And to have people like, looking at him? And they're thinking, I bet that car can go really fast? And then giving the gas just a little extra? When the light turns green? The tires? The sound they make? Well, that's pretty cool. Every time the babysitter babysits the children, he promises to take them out in the Firebird one day, but so far, his mother has dropped him off in the driveway in a light blue station wagon, while the Firebird, the babysitter says, is in the shop.

Whenever the babysitter babysits the children, he brings his own record albums—LPs, he calls them, a name the boy will later try out on his father, impressing him, where did you learn that?—and plays them on the parents' stereo. The children didn't know their stereo could get that loud, but it can, the babysitter would have them know. Listen to this! Check this song out! When the babysitter listens to LPs on the stereo, he pretends he's playing an instrument, a guitar, keyboard, or drums. Or he squints his eyes shut tight and pretends to sing into a phantom microphone, his free arm describing a circle in the air, like a windmill. Sometimes, the babysitter's eyes admit tiny tears, just at the corners. The babysitter wipes these away and fake-sings into the pretend microphone. Once, he forgets himself entirely and sings at the top of his tuneless voice. He clenches his fist, but the singer's last note escapes him. Still, the children clap. The babysitter bows, runs his hands through his hair. "You never heard a song like that before," he says and smiles. But what kind of song it is, the babysitter does not say.

After the children put themselves to bed, the babysitter comes into their room to say goodnight. Did they brush their teeth? For real? Sure you're not lying? OK, cool. Got to keep those choppers clean. Hey, what's this? the babysitter asks, but he's already holding the father's old coin savings bank, pulls the lever a few times. The boy explains how it works.

"Ten dollars?" the babysitter says, then whistles. "Man, that's gonna take forever."

"Yeah," the boy says. He hasn't put money in it since he found the dime.

"Here," the babysitter says, placing the bank on the boy's

dresser. "Tell you what. I'll make a donation." He fishes around in his jeans pockets.

"That's OK," the boy says. "You don't have to."

"I know it's in here somewhere," the babysitter says. He turns his front pockets inside out—the boy has never seen anyone actually do that before, ever—but they only produce a receipt, a ticket stub, and a black guitar pick, shiny as a polished stone. "Hey!" the babysitter exclaims. "I've been looking everywhere for this. I just about flipped my bedroom upside down trying to find it." He holds it up to the light. "Can't believe it was in my pocket the whole time." He strums an imaginary guitar with the found pick. "Isn't that hilarious?"

Is it hilarious? The boy isn't sure but says "yeah," just to be on the safe side.

———

BUT WHAT DO the parents do all day? Whenever the girl thinks about them, going to work and doing their jobs—the girl sees her mother at her desk, sees her father hanging his coat on the coat-rack that stands in the office entranceway, the office she and her brother visit more often now, since the separation, on those occasions when the father must bring them along—it is like trying to imagine what's beyond the ocean or the edge of the universe. When she was little, the girl liked to imagine the earth as seen from a distance, all hazy blue and green, and then imagine that distance widening, slowly, at first, the earth growing smaller and smaller, crowded out by other planets, stars, and then diminishing to a tiny dot, like the one the guest bedroom TV leaves whenever the girl turns it off, a perfect circle in the middle of the screen that burns brightly, defying everything, until it vanishes altogether.

What do her parents do all day?

GUMMA CALLS the children on the phone. The mother is already asleep on the family room sofa, so the children talk to Gumma alone, first the boy and then the girl. To the boy, Gumma says, "Do you know what I was doing just before I called you?" Before the boy can answer, Gumma says, "I was sitting here on my couch looking at that nice picture of the sunset someone special painted for me, and I thought, Now who was it who painted that pretty picture of the sunset for me? And then I remembered that my grandson painted that pretty picture of the sunset for me, and I said, You know what I'm going to do? I'm going to call that nice grandson of mine and tell him that I was just sitting here looking at that nice picture he painted for me and tell him I love him."

The boy, embarrassed, begins to explain that he did not paint that picture, but Gumma continues as if he's not there. "I love you," she says again. "Do you know that? I love you." Gumma laughs as if she's said something surprising, but the boy isn't sure if he's supposed to laugh too. "That's what I was doing before I called. I was sitting here in my house looking at that nice painting, thinking how much I love you, and then I just picked up that telephone and called you to tell you I love you."

"I love you too," the boy says, and his sister gives him a look. She's standing next to him, twirling the phone cord into knots, the way she's not supposed to.

"Do you know that?" Gumma says. "I love you."

The boy hands the phone to his sister, who says, "Hi Gumma, it's me." But the boy can tell Gumma isn't listening to his sister either. The boy watches his sister twirl the cord into thicker and thicker knots, fascinating tangles that hang from the cord like twisted apples. She nods her head, says, "I didn't paint that"; says,

"I love you too"; says, "Me too"; says, "Me too"; says, "I love you too"; says, "I have to go now, Gumma"; says, "We have to go now, Gumma"; says, "I love you too." Hangs up. Looks at her brother.

"The cord," he says.

The girl lets go of the cord, which she has twisted into so many knots that the action of the knots uncoiling lifts the phone receiver from its cradle and sends it crashing to the floor. The phone bounces, knocks against the linoleum. The children regard the fallen phone as if it were alive, some malevolent creature intending harm perhaps.

"Pick that up!" their mother says, materializing from the family room. Her hair sticks up from where she was sleeping on the sofa. "Pick up that phone right now!" She looks sleepy. She always looks sleepy.

But the children do not pick up the phone. Something has frozen them in place. And it isn't until their mother reaches down, grabs the phone, and places it back in the cradle, that they realize what it is: the tiny sound of Gumma saying, "I love you, I love you," from the phone's earpiece.

———

ONE NIGHT, the mother is studying for class when the cat appears at the sliding glass doors that lead from the kitchen to the deck. The cat puts its paws against the glass. Meows. The mother looks up from her notebook. The sight of the cat, brown fur mottled with gray, paws white and accusatory, rouses something in the mother she can't quite name. The cat blinks in the needy way it always used to, back when it was around the house more often. Dark briars cling to the cat's mangy undersides, a summer ritual. The mother's job, to comb them out, the cat resistant, resentful. The cat yawns its pink mouth.

"Go away," the mother says, and the cat eventually turns from the door and heads off into the night.

———

THE FATHER has left some of his records behind in case the children would like to listen to them. The girl doesn't want to listen to them but says that was nice of him. The boy doesn't want to listen to them either, but, bored one afternoon, goes through them anyway, dutifully, driven by guilt more than anything. Why does the boy so often feel guilty? Another mystery to place alongside his father's choice of records, nearly all classical, his father's music, boring, the kind he used to sing along to while washing dishes, moving his fingers in the air, conducting, the boy supposes, or playing an instrument. Either way, embarrassing. The boy settles on a record whose jacket shows a red-capped boy dragging a wolf by a rope. The boy knows this one, sort of; it's got a few loud parts where the drums get into it, so there's that, at least. He isn't allowed to use the record player by himself, his father's rule, but his father isn't here anymore, so, the boy figures, neither is the rule.

———

A POPULAR TREAT the summer the parents separate: Magic Shell chocolate syrup. Pour it over vanilla ice cream, wait two minutes, and voila, the chocolate has hardened, an ice cream bar requiring cracking. Use a spoon. See? It's like an Eskimo Pie? The children love Magic Shell. The mother thinks it's a waste of money but throws it in the shopping cart anyway.

———

GUMMA CALLS. The boy answers. Gumma tells the boy he needs to be careful not to grow up queer. That's something that can happen to boys from broken families, she says. "It's the lack of a male influence," she explains. "That's what does it."

The boy has no idea what Gumma is talking about. Tells her he will be careful.

"Just be on the lookout," she says.

The boy wants to ask what he should be on the lookout for, but Gumma tells him she has to put down the phone for a second, without quite saying, the boy dimly realizes, that she'll be back in just a second. The boy hears miscellaneous shuffling sounds, a microwave being turned on perhaps, then the unmistakable sound of a television, although the boy cannot tell which program. The boy waits. Minutes pass. The boy grows nervous; he's never hung up the phone without the other person saying goodbye first. What will happen if he hangs up the phone without the other person saying goodbye first? As if to answer his question, the boy hears Gumma's phone scrape against something—a countertop? the floor?—and then someone hangs up.

The boy says, "Bye."

———

DURING THE WEEK, the father goes to work and then returns to his apartment, where the children are not in the second bedroom, not reading the Hardy Boys and Nancy Drew mysteries in their respective beds, not waiting for him to rise and ask them what they want to do today, even though he knows what they're going to do today; they're going to go swimming, once he's had his coffee and checked the newspaper—they sometimes see a second movie on Saturday if it's raining outside—and once they've each had a second bowl of Frosted Flakes and whatever fruit he's managed not to forget (he's always throwing away the fruit he buys for the children, it seems, a bag of well-intended oranges starting to turn, each orange limned with green dross, or a bag of grapes, the only fruit his son will eat aside from bananas, which the father also ends up throwing away).

But the children are not there during the week. They are at home, of course, at their *mom's house*, what they've started calling what they used to call *home*: Mom's house. I think I left my toothbrush at Mom's house. We never get pizza at Mom's house anymore. These are the plates we used to have at Mom's house. *Home. House.* Separation divides words as easily as weeks into weekdays and weekends, single holidays into double holidays, like the girl's birthday, the last week of May, a party already in place before the father had moved out, so the parents uneasily agree that he will attend the party as planned. The party is princess-themed, but already that theme seems dated, too young for the girl now, who has seen her parents scream red-faced at each other—things they already regret, things the father must not think about late at night, if he is ever to find sleep—and who has comforted her mother as she cried in the checkout aisle, saying, in front of her brother, the clerk, and the young couple in line behind them, "Everything just keeps coming, whether you're ready for it or not."

The day of the party, the father arrives late. Events are already in full swing. He greets his daughter in the kitchen, where her mother has set a birthday cake on the table beside the gifts. His son is dutifully wearing his polo shirt, bored at this party of girls, embarrassed by these silver streamers, by this pink cake. The father gives him a playful tap on the shoulder; the boy puts his hands in his pockets. The children's mother takes a picture of the girl standing next to the cake. The children's mother takes a picture of the girl and her friends standing next to the cake. One more, she says. And another.

"You want to be in the next one?" the father asks his son, but his son only mumbles no. "You sure?" the father asks.

"Yeah," the son says.

"Boring party?"

"Yeah."

"Fun for your sister, though. Right?"

The boy shrugs. The girls have moved to the back deck to play Pin the Tail on the Donkey, but it's not even a donkey, it's a horse bearing a foolish grin.

"You want to head outside?" the father asks.

But the boy has done something strange: he has begun to cry. "Why are you here?" he asks.

THREE

NOW THAT HIS father has moved out, the boy feels he's been strangely promoted, although that's something he would never admit to anyone. Take this evening, for example. The downstairs toilet, always a problem toilet, has been refusing to flush since last night. Toilet paper swirls uselessly, like abject lilies in the bowl. The handle, pressed, raises the water level to near overflow, where it threatens to crest, then mysteriously abates, making a sound like a wind-guttered candle as it grudgingly exits. Why?

This is the kind of occasion where the father would be summoned. In fact, this occasion has always been the kind of occasion where the father has been summoned, and, as an unforeseen result of the father's moving to an apartment where, presumably, he has taken his toilet-fixing skills along with his power drill, the boy is now the one to take charge. Out of my way, the boy imagines saying, as he enters the bathroom. What's the situation? I'll take it from here. The boy lifts the heavy top of the toilet, as he has seen his father do, and places it across the sink. From the doorway, his mother tells him to be careful, but the boy can detect something he's starting to notice more and more often now: sometimes his parents say things to hear themselves say it, when, all along, they mean something closer to the opposite of what they've just said. It would be great if you could fix that toilet for us is closer to what his mother means to say. Otherwise, I'm going to have to pay someone.

"I can do it," the boy says, but his mother has left the doorway.

And the boy can do it. A few minutes later the toilet flushes properly, the toilet paper vanishes into the wherever. The water fills to the correct level. The boy replaces the heavy top, slides it into place, where it catches with a satisfying clunk. The boy washes his hands twice, a celebration. He enters the family room. His mother and sister are watching TV. A game show where contestants pull a long lever lit with tiny bulbs. The host wears a red tie and holds a microphone as slender as a marching baton.

"It's fixed," the boy announces.

"You fixed it?" his mother says.

"Yeah," the boy says.

"Thank you," his mother says. "That's a huge help."

"He didn't fix it," his sister says, but she does not look up. She watches the game show, where the contestant is hopping up and down.

"Be nice," his mother warns. "Your brother is turning out to be a real handyman."

"Whatever," his sister says. On TV, the contestant is standing inside a tornado of dollar bills. The contestant grabs and grabs at the money, but the money eludes her grip. The audience cheers. The contestant is wearing safety goggles. And that's the end of the conversation, because how could you not stop whatever it was you were talking about to watch that?

———

THE PRESIDENT is sad. You can tell just by looking at him. Even though he isn't the one who got in trouble for telling a lie and had to fly away on a helicopter; this is the one with the teeth who likes peanuts. Still, poor president, so sad. He says America has some problems that have no answers. He says America has lost its confidence. And he's right, the boy wants to tell him. The president should hear his mother crying herself to sleep at night.

ONE WEEKEND, the father tells the children he has a little surprise for them. The three of them have just gone out for their second movie of the weekend, one they've already seen before but agreed it would be fun to see again. The children cannot recall seeing the same movie twice at the theater, ever. A luxury of waste that thrills the two of them initially, seated among all these first-timers, who do not know, as the children do, what's about to happen next. But after a few anticipated twists, the children grow bored. The movie, at second glance, robbed of surprise, reveals itself to be a fantastic soundtrack dutifully accompanied by dialogue, action, and plot. A movie, viewed too closely, is a shoddy thing. The children ask their father whether they can leave early. Their father says, Are you sure? The children say they are sure. Outside, the sunlight is blinding, the air-conditioning in the father's car slow to cool.

On the ride home, the father says, "There's someone I want you two to meet."

Who? the children ask.

"A friend," the father says.

The girl shoots a look at the boy, who, the girl can tell, has no idea what her look means. The boy is a child. The boy has no idea about anything.

"A friend?" the girl says.

"Sarah," the father says.

"Sarah," the girl says, and the boy sees that his sister is on the verge of tears. Why? More and more, it seems, it's getting so that you never know when someone is going to start crying. "Who's Sarah?"

The father explains: Sarah is a new friend of his, someone he likes to spend time with. Someone who says she would very much like to meet the children — the father has told her so much about them—and someone they're really going to like getting to know, since it's always nice to get to know a new friend, isn't it? The boy nods. He agrees. Because how could you not agree that it's nice to meet a new friend, especially one who's heard so much about you and wants to meet you, too?

So why does his sister place her face in her hands and cry?

"A girlfriend," she says.

The father says no, a friend.

"Friend, girlfriend," the girl says.

"Friend," the father says, but the girl doesn't say anything. She is strange that way. Sometimes the boy will say something to her, and she won't say anything back, even though the boy knows she heard him. Whenever she does that, the boy feels like he's losing a game whose rules he doesn't even know.

The father tells them about Sarah. Sarah works in a restaurant where the father often likes to have lunch. That's how they met and became friends: the father went in for lunch and started talking to Sarah. Sarah is in graduate school, part-time, which means she doesn't go to school all the time, the way the children do, even though she is always studying for her exams, even in the summer, even as she works waiting tables and taking care of her mother, who is older and needs Sarah's help.

"I thought we could surprise Sarah," the father says.

"Surprise how?" the boy asks.

The father tells them. When he's finished, the girl says, "I won't do it."

But she does. The father drives them to the restaurant where Sarah works, a burger and ice cream place the children have been to once or twice before, the kind of restaurant where club sandwiches arrive impaled with glittering toothpicks, and the cash register supports a glass bowl of jellied mints the size of dice. As instructed, they enter the restaurant and ask for a table for three. "Our dad will be here in a few minutes," they explain to the hostess, whose look of indifference accompanies them to a booth by the window, where they can see into the parking lot, their father watching them from the car, windows down, parked in the shade.

"Your server will be with you shortly," the hostess says.

Through the window, the children can see their father watching them. They cannot see his expression, but the girl knows it is likely the one he wears whenever dessert is on the way, the moment before it arrives. My father is a fool, the girl thinks, but immediately feels guilty for thinking that. To compensate, she offers her father a sly wave. He waves back. There's such relief, the girl thinks, in knowing no one knows your thoughts.

A moment later, Sarah arrives. She is young and pretty, but not too pretty. Medium pretty, like their mom—another thought the girl is glad no one knows. She fills two tall glasses with water and says, "Are you two who I think you are?"

The children say they are. Sarah says it is nice to meet them. Pretty smile.

"And this was your father's idea?"

The children say yes, it was.

"And he's watching us right now from the parking lot?"

"Yeah," the girl says.

"He told us to," the boy explains.

"Hmm," Sarah says, "I see." She produces a notepad from her apron pocket and begins writing in it. "Well, I better take your order," Sarah says. To the girl she says, "I'm guessing you want a grilled cheese," and to the boy she says, "And you absolutely want a cheeseburger and fries."

"And a Coke," the boy says.

"And a Coke," Sarah says. "And I already wrote down your ginger ale," she says to the girl. "So that's all taken care of. Now, the next thing to do is to look really surprised when your father walks in. That seems like a good plan, right? What do you guys think?"

The children say that sounds like a good plan.

"Good. I think we can do it. We can look surprised."

The children say they can do it.

"Great," Sarah says. "Because he just walked through the door. But don't look. It'll be like I'm just taking your order. La-la-la. Here I am, taking your order."

The children nod. Someone is playing with sparklers inside the girl's stomach. Their father arrives at the booth, throws his arms open wide, and says, "What are you two kids doing here?"

Sarah and the children turn surprised faces on him, and then Sarah leans down into the girl's ear and says, "Good job."

———

THE COIN BANK is up to $3.20. The boy holds the bank, admiring its growing heft. What will he buy?

———

THE MOTHER takes the children to the state fair. Problem: they are not the kind of family that goes to the state fair. They are the kind of family that eats dinner in front of the TV. They are the kind of family that forgets to return library books, the overdue notices arriving with the regularity of utility bills. They are the kind of family that has not seen the family cat in nearly a month. They do not comprehend funnel cake. Funnel cake is a mystery to place alongside cotton candy, Tilt-A-Whirl, Skee-Ball, country music, tractor pulls, and face painting. So, is it any wonder that they avoid the petting zoo? Is it strange that they do not want to see a live monkey or touch a real live boa constrictor, as a pith-helmeted attendant invites them to do?

"She's three years old," the attendant says, brightly, "and you can visit her year-round at our zoo. Do you want to pet her?"

The mother gently urges the children behind her, her arm across the girl's chest, the way she sometimes does when she brings the car to a sudden stop. "Habit," she'll say.

"No thanks," the mother says.

"Maybe the children would like to?" the attendant says. The snake is a shimmering, heavy rope slung loosely around her shoulders. "She's a real sweetie."

"Listen," the mother says. "I don't want them touching that damn snake."

"Oh, I'm sorry," the attendant says, taken aback. "I didn't realize."

"You keep that snake away from me and my children."

"Ma'am, I'm very sorry—"

"If there's one thing I don't need right now, it's my children going around touching snakes."

"We wouldn't," the girl protests, too quiet to hear.

"Ma'am—"

"Because I've got to tell you, that's just about the last thing in the whole world that I need right now, it really is."

"I apologize if—"

But the mother has already steered them away, embarrassment settling on the boy and girl as heavily as the gray-green bib the dentist uses whenever he takes X-rays, the X-ray machine pointed to their open jaws, which always makes the children start to cry, just a little, even as the dentist says, "You're doing great."

———

ONE DAY, the girl hears her brother fooling around on the piano. He plays "Chopsticks" and the first few measures of "Heart and Soul" before the song gets ahead of him. He stops. What else can he play? "Jingle Bells," but only during the holidays—he's weird about hearing Christmas music out of season. If the girl even attempts the opening groove of "Linus and Lucy," her brother will yell at her to stop. Threaten to close the piano lid on her fingers. Now, she listens as her brother presses the pedals, hits a couple of stray notes here and there, moving lower and lower on the keyboard, until he reaches the lowest note and plays it over and over again, a mournful dirge. Doom, doom, doom.

It occurs to the girl that her brother plays as if no one is listening, even though he must realize she's in the house and can hear him now, playing the same low note over and over again. He knows that, of course, but he also doesn't know it. The note sounds through the house a dozen times, in slower and slower intervals. How foolish her brother is, the girl thinks, playing the piano as if no one can hear him. How embarrassing it is to listen to someone else playing the piano in another room—is that the way she sounds to others when she plays? Yes, it must be. A truth as awful as realizing you are a part of everything you experience and that other people see you and hear you and recognize you in ways you rarely recognize yourself, you aware-yet-unaware of your presence in the world, a spell that is occasionally broken by photographs: there she is in the most recent class photo, hair in two embarrassing pigtails, hands folded atop her knees, mouth still deciding whether to smile, when the photographer looked up from behind the camera and said, "Say, 'No homework!'" and captured the girl with her mouth slack, eyes closed.

This week, when the piano teacher arrives, the girl says she's decided to quit. "I'm sorry," she says. "I hope you're not too mad." And the girl is disappointed when the teacher doesn't try to talk her out of it.

THERE'S A MAN who rides a bicycle around the father's parking lot. The girl sees him sometimes, when the three of them are returning from wherever, the parking lot otherwise empty aside from this fifty-something, overweight, undershirted, sunburned rider, sporting camo pants, black boots, and a baseball cap whose logo has been torn off. A milk crate rests between the bicycle's handlebars, affixed with fraying bungee cords. The crate shelters a few dozen soda cans, dented, crushed, gleaming. The man's face is red and raw looking, his expression impossible to read. He does not acknowledge them on those few occasions when he passes by just as they are stepping from the car. Nor do they acknowledge him, which the girl might typically find strange if she didn't feel uncertain and uneasy about him, which her father and brother must feel too, as they never say anything when the bicycle man passes by, never mention him whatsoever. But one time the girl meets his eyes, those blank apertures, and the man is looking back at her. And, although it is unfair, and although the girl knows it is not the kind of thing she should think about the man riding the bicycle, when his eyes catch hers, her thoughts admit a word they normally would not let pass.

Perv, the girl thinks.

THE MOTHER works two evenings and three days a week. Classes two nights a week, Tuesdays and Thursdays. The children spend the weekend at their father's apartment—or not. It depends. Sometimes the mother packs the children's bags and the father calls at the last minute and says this weekend is no good, sorry. When that happens, the mother tells the children she's decided to take them to her parents' house or to church—the children only go to church with their mother, not their father.

This weekend, their father drives them to church, parks in the parking lot but doesn't leave the car. "Your mother made me promise to take you to church this weekend," he explains, "so here I am taking you to church this weekend." He unlocks the doors and rolls down the windows. "I'll wait for you here." He reclines his seat—a sudden clunking noise—and closes his eyes. "Ah," he says. "This is *my* kind of church." He laughs. Outside, cars pull into other spots, parents with kids in tow, old people and more old people, the men in ill-fitting jackets, the women clutching white purses. "You may go or you may stay," the father says, his eyes still closed, "and I will only tell your mother that I took you to church just like I promised. I want to leave it entirely up to you since I feel that you are both getting old enough now to make decisions for yourselves. That's something important to me, to see you making your own decisions." He opens his eyes for a moment to see if his words are registering with the children, but they only stare at him blankly: is he really going to let them skip church?

"We don't have to go?" the boy asks.

"You may or you may not," the father says. "I leave it up to you."

"Mom wouldn't like that," the girl says.

"If you want me to tell her what I offered you, I will," the father says. He leans back on the headrest. "I don't want to break my promise to your mother so much as I want you two to have the option of thinking for yourselves. Does that make sense?"

It does not make sense. "That makes sense," the boy says.

"She told us to go," the girl says.

"Then you should go," the father says.

"Come on," the girl says. She opens her door. "Let's go."

"But Dad said—"

"That's what I think parenting is all about," the father says, "teaching your children to think for themselves. Giving your kids a chance to make their own choices. And you know what? It's kind of fun, making up your own mind." He turns a hopeful yet strange smile on them, the one that crops up more often now that Sarah is in the picture. "I think you're going to like making your own decisions. Feeling more like a grown up. I still remember the day my dad let me choose whether I wanted to try out for baseball. Did you know I used to play baseball? Anyway, I knew I was no athlete—that's for sure!—but I'd always thought playing baseball was something I was supposed to want to do, even though, deep down, I didn't really like playing on a team. Know what I liked? I liked throwing a tennis ball against the garage door and catching it with my fielder's mitt. I could play that for hours, but standing in the outfield inning after inning, waiting for someone to hit one my way? Well, no thanks. Not for me."

"I'm going in," the girl says, opening the passenger door.

"OK," the father says, "that's your decision."

"I'm staying," the boy says.

"No you're not," the girl says.

"Am too," the boy says. The boy and girl repeat this exchange until the father says, "Enough. You've each made your own decision. Your sister will go to church, and we'll wait outside."

"But—" the boy says.

"End of story."

The father tells the girl they'll wait for her here until mass is over. They're not going anywhere, he says. "We'll be right here." The girl detects the boy's look of hesitation: he didn't realize his father planned to wait in the parking lot. He is about to speak when he realizes, as the girl already has, that waiting in the parking lot might be boring, yes, but it is still preferable to going to church. "Have fun," he says, "at church." The girl shuts the car door without a word. Reminds herself not to look back. Angry when she turns to see her brother not watching her.

Inside the church, the girl realizes three things: she is late, she will look out of place sitting by herself, and she doesn't really want to go to church at all. But turning back would mean handing her brother an easy victory. And her father would likely celebrate her choosing to back out of her first choice, so forget that. The church, a more modern-looking building than the church they attend with their mother, gives off a whiff of incense and carpet cleaner. The opening hymn is just concluding as the girl scans the pews for an open spot. A family of four slides in to make room for her, but before the girl can say no thank you, another family arrives behind her, a mother with two toddlers, one crying, the other clutching a cheap, joyless coloring book, and the girl must take the offered seat. The girl makes the same inner pledge she makes every week at the start of mass, to pay attention this time, a pledge she's failed by the first reading. Who cares if she goes to church or not? Her mom, that's who. But her mom will never know. Only if her brother tells, which he won't. And if her mother asks if she went to church, the girl can honestly say yes, and if the mother asks how was it, she could honestly say it was fine, she guesses. What about God? Yes, good question. What about Him anyway?

When the congregation stands for the reading from scripture, the girl mumbles excuse me, sorry, and makes her way to the exit and then outside to the parking lot, where this day is shaping itself up quite nicely into one fine day, the sun rising high, the air redolent of honeysuckle and lilies, the trees bordering the parking lot sending a latticework of shadows across the asphalt, a map of interconnecting lines so intriguing the girl's eyes could get lost in them as she waits for her father and brother, who have not waited outside for her after all, and who pull into the parking lot twenty minutes later and see her standing in the lattice shadows and slow their car into a parking space, the radio blaring. Her brother holds a white bag out the passenger window.

"We got McDonald's!" he says.

FOUR

HERE'S SOMETHING that's sort of nice: for years, the boy felt scared whenever his parents went out for the night and left them with a babysitter. As the night wore on, the boy would grow afraid that his parents would not return all. Maybe they had been killed in a car crash. Maybe they had disappeared with no explanation whatsoever. Maybe they would vanish and there would be a memorial service for them, and when the boy attended the memorial service he wouldn't know how to act, and everyone would think what a terrible son he was for not acting the right way at his parents' memorial service, everyone's disapproval as clear and obvious as the boy's failure to cry the way you'd expect a boy to cry at his parents' memorial service.

The nice part? Now that his parents don't go out together anymore, the boy doesn't have to worry about that.

———

ONE EVENING, the father arrives early to pick the children up for the weekend and must wait a few minutes in the foyer while the mother helps the children find socks and shirts from all the piles of clothes strangely stacked on the stairs, leaving only one side of the stairway accessible. The father's thought: how nice to leave this mess behind.

———

THE MOTHER keeps a pair of scissors in the kitchen drawer beneath the microwave. The children use the scissors for homework assignments, craft projects, gift wrapping (although the boy cannot wrap a present to save his life and must ask his sister to do it for him), opening packages, cutting labels from cans (their grandmother saves them for reasons the children aren't curious enough to ask), poking holes in lids, or opening tricky bags of frozen vegetables, their corners refusing to tear. The scissors are heavy, old. Dull. The mother keeps saying she's going to sharpen them one day, but she never does. How do you sharpen scissors?

To cut wrapping paper, you must stretch the paper taut, otherwise the scissors will tear the paper rather than cut the paper, the girl explains.

The boy likes to cut grape stems with the scissors. The way the stem resists, then yields, the scissors closing tight. Ah!

The mother has shown them the proper way to hand someone a pair of scissors: first, you close the scissors and hold them not from the handle but from the blades, closed tight, secure; next, you extend your opposite hand and turn it flat so that the other hand may place the scissors across the top, as gently as possible, a show of safety, respect, and care.

Even as their mother cries herself to sleep some nights, even as the lawn grows as high as the boy's socks, and even as the girl slams her bedroom door whenever she's been banished to her room, the three of them continue to hand each other the scissors with the regality and decorum of a coronation.

———

ON A NIGHT the children are home alone, Gumma calls. "Where'd your mother go?" she says.

The boy says she has school tonight.

"And left you all alone?"

The boy says they can go to bed by themselves.

"Check underneath," Gumma says. "First."

SOMETIMES, when the children spend the weekend with their father, Sarah joins them for dinner. After the father picks the children up at their mother's house, he asks them if it would be OK if Sarah came with them to dinner? He tells them he won't be angry if they say no; in fact, he'd understand it if they say no. That's something he understands completely. It is. That's something he wants them to know: no matter what they choose, he will understand their choice, without any anger or resentment or misgivings or loss of love and affection. OK?

"Fine by us," the boy says.

The girl says, "I guess so."

"Super," the father says. Then, "But it would have been super if you said no too. OK?"

When they arrive at the restaurant, though, Sarah is already there. Waiting at the bar. "Hi guys," she says. "I kept thinking I saw you three coming in through the door, even if the people didn't really look like you. I would stand up and get ready to say hi, and then realize it wasn't really you. Then I'd sit back down until it happened again." Sarah laughs. "Isn't that kind of funny?"

"Yeah," the children agree.

The father gives Sarah an ordinary hug, that's how the girl thinks of it, an ordinary hug that will yield to a romantic one by the time Sarah returns with them to the apartment. "Well, it's really us this time," the father says. "See?"

"Does that ever happen to you?" Sarah says, addressing the children. Something the girl really likes about Sarah: she never forgets she's speaking to them too.

"Uh-huh," the boy says.

"Sometimes," the girl says.

"Really? Wow, that makes me feel a little better. I thought I was probably the only one that happened to. Whew, OK. Thanks."

After dinner, they go to an animated movie that's too young for the children, but the children don't say anything. They play along, laugh when they should laugh, feign interest in the too-long musical numbers, suck soda from thick straws, twist napkins into pieces and leave the pieces on the floor. The girl watches her father, the way the light catches in the corners of his glasses. From time to time, Sarah will lean in and whisper something in his ear, something that makes him laugh. Something funny. Sarah is funny, there's no getting around it. The girl gets why her dad likes Sarah, but as soon as the thought arrives, she feels like she must chase it away. On the screen, a hippopotamus is playing piano on a zebra's black-and-white hide. Bright birds perch on the hippo's head, their beaks swaying in time to the music. Monkeys swing from colorful vines. The birds sing.

———

A SECRET THE boy keeps and will keep forever: he heard the crash that killed those teenagers. He did. At least he thinks so. He remembers it, even if he can't remember it exactly. What he remembers is lying in bed with his window open and his fan blowing on him, turning the way his fan does, that sound it makes like it's trying to tell him something, the boy can't say what, even though the boy knows the fan really isn't trying to say anything. A fan is just a fan. His room is just his room. His open window is just his open window, and the cars passing on the roads outside to wherever are just cars passing on the roads outside to wherever.

Except for that night. The boy heard something. A sound like two shopping carts slipping into one another. The boy sat up in bed; he remembers that. Maybe he was asleep and the sound woke him up. Maybe he was awake and the sound kept him from falling asleep. Or was the sound more like the one his fan makes? Either way, the boy heard something.

Maybe.

———

IT'S RIDICULOUS, the mother thinks, the way the father now dons sneakers, T-shirts, and jeans, always a no-no in their married days, the father sometimes mowing the lawn in khakis and a polo. Did the mother actually witness him pulling into the driveway with his car windows down, his arm slung loosely atop the panel, nonclassical music blaring from speakers that hitherto only knew Schubert and NPR? She did, the father's sunglasses would have her know, peeking stupidly from his windblown hair.

———

WELL, THE BOY can cut the grass, can't he? The boy's mother is doubtful. She tells the boy she will hire someone to do it. The babysitter maybe. The mother is watching TV. The mother is tired.

The boy says he can do it. Well, he can do everything except start the mower. But maybe if she could start the mower for him? The mother says she will think about it. The mother is watching the local news. On the local news, an old man in overalls is telling a young reporter about his vegetables. Squash. Corn. The young man nods at the old man, laughs, asks him questions about this vegetable or that, but the boy can tell he's not really paying attention, not totally. Adults are good at that.

So, the boy asks, you'll start the mower?

The mother sighs. "I'll do it at the next commercial," she says.

But at the next commercial, the mother is asleep. On TV, people are terribly excited about what's happening at a car dealership. Should the boy wake her? At the dealership, it's raining bright balloons. The sight of his mother sleeping makes up the boy's mind for him, the way it sometimes does.

The boy rolls the push mower into the front yard, where the grass is slickly wet, tall as the boy's tube socks. A T-shaped cord grows from the mower's head; the boy grabs the cord, as he has done dozens of times before, and pulls, but the mower refuses to start. The boy tries again, even though he knows the mower will not start. Sometimes the boy feels like he's performing for an audience, an audience that's watching him now, wanting to witness his good effort, even though the boy knows that's ridiculous, there's no audience. Still, the boy pulls the cord and wipes nonexistent sweat from his forehead.

And it isn't until the boy rolls the mower back onto the driveway that he realizes it's the tall, wet grass that's keeping the blade from turning, which, in the boy's sudden understanding of the mower's simple mechanics, is what's keeping the mower from starting. "Oh," the boy says, to appease the audience. "I get it now."

When the mower starts, a plume a gray smoke rises from the engine and seems to follow the boy into the yard.

———

SARAH WANTS the girl to confide in her, that's something the girl can tell about Sarah but won't reveal. Better to keep it a secret, see where it leads. The truth is that the girl likes Sarah but isn't sure if it's OK to feel that way since, among other obstacles, the girl's mother has instructed her not to get too close to Sarah. "Just passing through," is the mother's estimation, a phrase the girl thinks about now, as she and Sarah go out on an errand together: they must find something to make for dinner tonight.

"Plus a nightlight," the girl says.

"Oh, right," Sarah says, "that's a good idea."

Last night, the boy kept asking for the nightlight their father usually kept in the bathroom, but after a search that included removing all of the towels from the linen closet outside the bathroom—their father uses the old towels the children last recall as toddlers, their yellow daisies summoning half-memories of their mother working the towel through their shampooed hair—they couldn't find the nightlight anywhere. The boy said he could sleep without it. Said it was no big deal really. He just thought if they had the nightlight, they might as well plug it in, you know? The boy's face showed an expression of absolute fear, mostly from his determination to show none.

"I could feel his nightmares," Sarah says.

"Ha," the girl says.

"Something about the invisible man and a playground," Sarah says. "Or maybe it was an invisible playground?"

"And an ordinary man," the girl says.

"That's it!" Sarah laughs. "He was just an ordinary man," Sarah intones, a movie trailer voice-over, "in an invisible playground, until one day. Everything. Changed."

The girl laughs her embarrassing laugh, the one that exposes her gums the way she doesn't like. The girl has been practicing laughing without exposing her gums, but sometimes she forgets.

"Your poor brother," Sarah says.

"He's annoying," the girl says.

But Sarah doesn't say anything. She liberates a shopping cart from another shopping cart and places her purse in the toddler seat, the same way the girl's mother does whenever they go to the supermarket. Sarah and the girl shop. They talk. The girl feels her heart going out a little bit to Sarah, a strange tug she isn't sure what to do with. They tour the produce aisle. They agree to buy tangerines because tangerines are so good and because Sarah is trying to eat better. "Want to stay in shape?" Sarah says. "Don't work where ice cream is free." They talk about lettuce. They forget about the nightlight until they are in the checkout aisle, and then they ask where the nightlights are, and the girl runs to get one, deciding, in an instant, on one shaped like a seashell over one where Snoopy is slumbering atop his doghouse. It is a boring nightlight, dull. But for the rest of the summer, it will preside in the apartment hallway, illuminating the path to the bedroom on those nights when the girl cannot sleep and wanders to the bathroom for a drink and a few moments of solitude, when she can practice smiling without showing her gums in the bathroom mirror.

———

QUESTION: why do people wait in line for gas if waiting in line for gas uses up more gas?

Answer: the boy has no idea. He watches them, car after car of angry adults. Windows down, even though there is no breeze. When one car advances, another takes its spot. Hands appear from windows, signaling malice. Drivers sound horns, make gestures, check rearview mirrors again and again. The lines grow. The air is heavy with exhaust.

———

THE MOTHER'S secret: she often looks forward to the children's going off to their father's apartment for the weekend. She does. She can't help it, is what she would say if anyone asked, but no one has asked, so the mother's secret congregates with the few she's garnered in the past few months—when did her life become so uninteresting? True, she's free of her marriage, free of her husband's sullen moodiness, his self-absorption, free of costarring in the little movie that forever played inside his head, the one where he quietly endured her indifference, noble husband, as she drifted into her own malaise, her own silence, her own refusal to accept her part in the marriage's demise, or whatever it was she had done to fail him, the marriage. Ah, gone, all of that. Goodbye sour anger and resentment; but what to fill her days with now? Separation has demoted her from a full-time parent to part-time, while making seasonal work of it for her ex. Weekends now offer up laundry, church, and housecleaning, as equally as they offer neglecting laundry, church, and housecleaning.

The mother drinks coffee while listening to the little kitchen radio she never listens to when the kids are around. Oldies, mostly, but sometimes classical or even talk programs, if she can stand them. If she can't find anything, then off with the radio. Because it is her choice, whether she wants to listen or not. Aha — how had she forgotten the feeling of doing what she wants? Parenting, despite its pleasures, now revealed itself, in the new and not quite flattering light of separation, as a series of affirmative answers to the question, What is the last possible thing in the world I want to do right now? Fix dinner for four. Sort clothes into lights and darks. Remind the children to stop leaving peanut butter knives in the sink. Enthuse about an improvised puppet show. Rinse yet another unrinsed milk glass. Feign confidence, optimism, delight.

Today, the mother is going to throw out those ratty-looking puppets she's been meaning to throw out since forever, since that's the kind of day the mother has decided today is. Plus, she's going to donate her ex's old ski boots. She's gotten tired of asking him when he's going to take those old ski boots. She heaves the ski boots into a white garbage bag to keep the puppets company.

———

WHEN THE CHILDREN return from another weekend at their father's, their mother says she has something to tell them. Great, the girl thinks. Whenever an adult tells you they have something to tell you — run. Run fast! Run fast and keep running!

"What's so funny?" the mother asks.

"Nothing," the girl says.

"You're kind of smiling," the boy says.

But the girl doesn't say anything. You could just not say anything forever and what could anyone do about it?

The mother tells them they will be spending next week at Grandmom and Grandpop's. Why? Because Grandmom and Grandpop would like to see them, of course. Why do Grandmom and Grandpop want to see them? Because Grandmom and Grandpop always want to see them, even if they have a hard time expressing it sometimes. Why does it have to be a whole week? Because Grandmom and Grandpop want to take them out to the club. No! Not the club. How the children hate the club, a church gymnasium fitted out with folding chairs and card tables, redolent of basketballs and holy water, where, the last time they visited, the boy won a toaster cozy in a raffle, and a top-hatted magician clumsily produced a nickel from the girl's ear.

"Well, I'm sure they have other things planned too," the mother says. "They'll just be happy having you two to themselves for a while."

But whether the grandparents have other things planned or are just happy having the children around is hard to say. By the end of the first day, the only thing the grandparents seem to have planned is watching TV in a room darkened by closed blinds, the sun is the enemy, their grandmother says, even though she must hold her crossword puzzle inches from her face. The grandfather naps in his recliner, his glasses askew, the television light giving the girl a sudden primer in what the word "bifocals" means. For supper they have tomato soup and sandwich bread, the bread tearing whenever the boy tries to butter it, the butter frozen, resisting his knife, which clanks the butter dish whenever the boy tries to urge it through.

"Here," his sister says, commandeering the knife. "You're doing it wrong."

"Am not," the boy says, forgetting to hide his lack of conviction.

"You press down too hard," the girl explains.

For dessert, they have vanilla ice cream with chocolate syrup. A consolation: even the incorrect brand of vanilla ice cream and no-frills chocolate syrup still tastes pretty good. Another: the grandparents seem to have no idea of what a child-sized portion looks like, and joylessly pile their bowls high, as if their ambition were to rid the house of ice cream as quickly as possible. The children eat in silence, even when the grandparents, each finished with their ice cream, rise from the table, rinse their bowls in the sink and shuffle into the family room to watch *Family Feud*. The boy looks at his sister, who has already given up on her bowl. "I can't finish this," she says.

"Me neither," the boy says, even though he was going to try before his sister said something. The kitchen, absent of the grandparents' breathing, lets the children in on a secret: there's a clock above the refrigerator shaped like a jack-o'-lantern that's been watching them the whole time.

Later in the week, the grandparents take the children to the club. The club is decorated with paper streamers and red-white-and-blue tablecloths, even though the Fourth of July is still weeks away. American flags hang from the club's stippled ceiling. From the front of the room, a man in a bow tie and suspenders calls a bingo game, his voice booming through the hall. B16! The grandmother takes the children from table to table but forgets to introduce them to her friends, or maybe she never really planned on introducing them in the first place? Instead, the grandmother speaks about them as if they are there but not really there either. The girl stands beside her brother, who seems to be following the bingo game with rapt and embarrassing attention. What if he never grows up?

"I've got my grandkids with me this week," the grandmother

is saying. "They come from a broken home. It's a shame. I said to my daughter, You know these kids are coming from a broken home now? I said, It's a shame. She says, Don't say that, but I said, It's the truth. Everyone will know they come from a broken home now. It's a shame."

"That is a shame," a woman agrees. The woman has three bingo cards in front of her, none with B16, though, the girl notices.

"It is," the grandmother says. "It's a shame. I said to my daughter, I said, You made a promise to God, remember that? And she got mad at me. She says, Mom, you don't understand, and I said, I understand all right. I understand it's a shame. It's a shame when people break their promises to God."

"That is a shame," another woman says. She gives the children a pitying look. Your glasses are slipping off, the girl thinks.

G43!

"And now these kids are going to grow up in a broken home," the grandmother says, and then clicks her tongue. "It's a shame. Some people don't realize what a shame some things are. I said to my daughter, I said, Everyone just wants to do whatever they want to do anymore. I said, Where's that going to get us, everyone just doing whatever they want to do? I said, No one wants to do what they're supposed to anymore; everyone just says, Me, me, me. But my daughter said, Mom, you don't know what you're talking about, but I know what I'm talking about all right. It's a shame, what I'm talking about."

At the next table, two women in straw hats sit alongside a woman sleeping in a wheelchair. The straw-hat women say hello to the children and ask them how old they are, but before the children can answer, the grandmother says, "They're staying with us for the week. They come from a broken home. It's a shame." One of the straw-hat women says to the boy, "You look like a nice strong young man. You could grow up to be a security guard. I have a son who used to be a security guard. He's passed now. Forty-two years old." The straw-hat woman snaps her frightening fingers. "Gone! Just like that. Forty-two. Left behind my daughter-in-law and three beautiful grandchildren."

"It's a shame," the grandmother says.

"It is," the straw-hat woman says. "One day he was going off to work, and the next day they were taking him away in an ambulance. Heart attack. And he was a big, strong man. Healthy."

"Shame," the grandmother says.

"He was always going for a run. That's what he always used to say. He'd come over to my place and bring the grandkids, and then he'd say, 'I'm going for a run,' and then he'd come back an hour later, and I'd say, Don't leave those shoes in the kitchen like you did last time; if you're going to leave those shoes here, you leave those shoes in the garage next to your father's old golf shoes. I said, I put those old golf shoes out in case you want them. Well, he didn't want them."

N31!

The woman in the wheelchair wakes, checks her bingo card, and places a chip on N31. Falls back asleep. The children's grandfather does that sometimes too. Sometimes, he'll just be sitting there watching TV with them, and the next thing the children know, he's asleep, like falling asleep is nothing at all. Another thing he does is belch and then say, Excuse me. Even if he's sleeping. They spend entire afternoons this way, the grandfather sleeping, the TV fuzzily conveying Bugs Bunny into the grandparents' living room, while the children slip deeper into boredom and loneliness, a subtle despair broken only by the grandfather's *Excuse me.*

When the grandchildren return to the grandfather's table, the grandfather shows them he nearly has bingo on two different cards. This excites the boy. The boy likes to win. Winning is good, great even. That's something the boy has always felt about winning, even if it's just winning bingo. He wants this win, he does. And the grandfather nearly wins on both cards, each one freckled with so many colored chips the grandfather cannot possibly lose, but he does lose; he loses to the woman in the wheelchair, who receives a jar of apple butter topped with a fat red bow, a prize the boy tells himself he never wanted anyway, no matter how good apple butter is.

FIVE

BUT SUMMER is so boring. It is. People like to believe in summer, the girl thinks, on more than one summer morning when she's idly eating Frosted Flakes in front of the TV, but what people really believe in isn't summer; it's the *idea* of summer. A loose compound of movies, TV shows, books, songs, vague feelings, and poor memory. But maybe most things are like that, this morning's Frosted Flakes would like the girl to know, these flakes crunchier, sugarier, and more milk-resistant than yesterday's, and more willing to let her in on some things they hadn't been letting her in on before. Like the TV program she's watching now, the one with the funny host who's pretending not to understand how to flip pancakes as the guest chef keeps laughingly trying to show him? Well, here's the thing: not only does the host completely understand how to flip pancakes, as the girl probably already guessed, but he also doesn't care about the right way to flip pancakes or the guest chef or cooking really. The host wants people to laugh. That's all. Anything else the girl might wish to think about the show—here's a good way to flip pancakes; talk shows teach you how to do things you didn't know how to do before—is just an *idea* of what's actually happening, not what's actually happening.

A terrifying thought chased away by the cat, who appears at the sliding glass doors and rubs his body against the panes.

"Here, kitty-kitty," the girl says. "Psst, psst!"

The boy, hearing her, runs into the living room. "Where is he?"

"At the doors," the girl says.

The boy's secret: sometimes he imagines talking to the cat, even when the cat isn't around. Imagines the cat understands him, this absent kitty does. This cat has got a firm grasp of all that troubles the boy, all his worries, doubts, fears, and anxieties. Those are all like the gift wrap the boy used to crumple into balls and toss the cat's way on Christmas morning. Thwap! the cat said to those.

The boy says, "Here, kitty-kitty!" and dashes to the doors.

But the cat has already run away.

———

SOMETIMES THE father has trouble sleeping at night. Sarah tells him to try turning his thoughts off, but the father can't turn his thoughts off, especially the ones that visit him on nights like tonight, with the children at their mother's house and Sarah beside him, her breathing deep and steady, Sarah a sound sleeper, as he discovered early on, the father able to make two trips to the bathroom without waking her. Tonight, the father returns to bed, his thoughts reeling. Options: spend the night on the couch watching TV. Wake Sarah. Don't wake Sarah. Spend night searching for sleep. Spend night searching for sleep while imagining conversation with Sarah. Imagined conversation it is.

Sarah?

Hey.

You awake?

Not personally.

Sorry.

What time is it?

Late. Early, I mean.

Oh.

I can't sleep.

I am increasingly aware of that.

Sorry.

Stop saying sorry. Say the thing you are going to say.

The thing about life being about everything I used to know plus possibility?

Yes.

It will feel good to say it.

Yes.

OK. I think what happened to me was, for as long as I could remember, life seemed like it was about everything I knew: my family, my job, my experience, my history—

Your wife.

Yes, my wife.

You weren't going to include her on your list.

No, I wasn't.

You weren't sure how I would react.

Right.

How I would react is I would think it cowardly of you not to include your wife on the list of everything you know, since your wife was—is—a huge part of your life, the mother of your children, and someone eminently worthy of mention in this imagined conversation.

OK.

Put her on the list.

OK. My history, *my wife*, my home, my childhood, my, well, everything, plus the possibility of everything else that I did not know, that was not part of my experience but somehow might become a part of it eventually.

I'm not sure I get that.

It's hard to explain.

Do you ever think about checking your thoughts before you think them? Like, Do I really believe the things I'm thinking, or do I just wish to believe them?

Usually, I just think and believe them.

Hmm.

So: possibility. My life always seemed like it had this tint of possibility around it.

Tint?

I think that's what I mean. I think. I was always aware of that feeling of possibility, even if I didn't realize that I was aware of it until it was gone. I think that's what happened. Life felt like it was only about the things I already knew and wouldn't be about possibility anymore. And I think I sort of panicked.

And I'm the result of your panic? Great, thanks.

No. My panicking didn't lead to you; my panicking led to me moving out, to the separation.

Which led to me.

No. That's not it.

That's absolutely it.

No.

Your conversation isn't going very well. You realize that, right?

I'm only trying to say that what I understood to be life as I knew it suddenly changed from everything I knew plus possibility to only everything I knew and nothing else.

The end of possibility?

The end of possibility.

I do not find this conversation especially convincing.

Sorry.

Goodnight.

———

THE NEXT TIME Gumma calls, the girl tells her she doesn't have time to talk right now, she's busy with something. Gumma says the girl is ten years old, what could she be so busy with that she doesn't have time to talk to her grandmother? The girl says,

"Things." Gumma laughs, says the girl is growing up fast. She'll grow up faster now, because of everything, that's a fact. No getting around it. The girl says she has to go.

Gumma says, "Your childhood is over."

―――――

SOMETIMES SARAH tells the children stories. The children listen, especially the girl, who is beginning to understand something about separation: when things separate, they double. So, where the children formerly had one home, they now have their mother's house and their father's apartment. Where they once had one kitchen table, they now have two. Where they once had one family history, they now have two, which includes Sarah, who grew up in Ohio, a state the children have never been to, and who likes to recall her childhood—as their mother, for example, does not—and whose stories are the kind the girl enjoys, the kind that start in the middle, with everything already in full swing, and tell you embarrassing and funny things and somehow make fun of the world all while convincing you that the world is a pretty terrific place nonetheless. Sarah is good at that kind of story; the girl is a good listener. Here is a story Sarah tells the children one night at dinner:

"When I was in third grade, there was a boy in my class who used to go from desk to desk, asking everyone whether they believed that his father went to school with Frank Gifford. If you said, Sure, I believe you, he would move on to the next desk and ask the same question again until someone would say, No, I don't believe your father went to school with Frank Gifford, and then the boy would work himself up into tears—he did this thing where he blinked his eyes like crazy and clenched his fists as tight as possible—and then he'd say, Why don't you believe that my father went to school with Frank Gifford? and then his mouth would twist in this weird way and then he'd just start bawling, Why don't you believe my father went to school with Frank Gifford? I've never seen anyone cry so hard. Then he would move on to the next desk and ask the same question again. He did that every day. I don't remember his name."

Another story to add to all the ones the girl already knows: the time their father took their mother to a double-header baseball game and their mother asked, after the first game was over, who the team would play next; the time the mother almost shook John F. Kennedy's hand; the time their great-grandpop put a dishtowel in their father's mouth when their father was a toddler and wouldn't stop crying because of what happened to Dumbo's mommy; the time their father, then nine years old, plugged in the Christmas tree at the exact same moment a drunk driver hit the family mailbox outside. How the father burst into tears, thinking it was somehow his fault.

Now the girl can add Sarah's schoolmate to the rest, leaving him to wander the classroom, which the girl has fitted out with posters, and caps and coats on pegs, because the girl can do that if she wants to.

———

SHOULD THE father ask the mother why she lets the boy mow the yard? Should the father offer to knock down the wasp nest growing inside the porch light fixture? Is the garage door coming off the track again? Is the woodpile in need of stacking? Is the father still the father?

———

IT ISN'T AS IF the boy doesn't have *any* friends, the boy would like to point out. It isn't like that at all. If someone were to say that the boy doesn't seem to have any friends, well, that person would be wrong because—and sometimes the boy makes a case of explaining this to the audience that always seems to congregate most heavily on those summer afternoons when he's deciding whether to venture outside and toss a deflated football to an imaginary receiver—the boy does have friends, except they're more like neighborhood *acquaintances*, is how he would put it. Does that make sense? Like Alan Decker? Let's take Alan Decker, for example. Now Alan is a few years older than the boy, sure, and lives on the opposite side of the neighborhood, but does that stop Alan from occasionally inviting the boy to be the scorekeeper whenever Alan swipes the boy's football from him and throws it to Chris Mauro—another acquaintance—on one of those afternoons when the two of them are biking past the boy's house just as he's kicked off to a phantom player? Or how about when Alan and Chris invite the boy to bring them some iced tea while the two of them take turns punting the ball over the boy's house, scoring ten points for a clean kick and five for a one-hop off the roof's weather-damaged shingles? How Alan and Chris preen whenever the boy applauds their best efforts, go Alan, awesome punt, Chris! How honored the boy feels whenever Alan and Chris allow him to retrieve the punts that carom oddly off the chimney and tumble into the Larson's yard, requiring the boy to ascend the tall-but-shaky fence that divides their property, then jump down into the Larson's yard, which always makes his feet do this weird thing where they feel like they're sort of on fire for a millisecond.

What the boy would like everyone to know is that Alan and Chris are *implied friends*. That's what everyone should know. Alan and Chris like spending time with the boy, even if it's just to ask how his summer is going, and could he bring them more of those Nutter Butters he brought them last time? So it's a not a big deal really, if sometimes the boy likes to imagine Alan and Chris watching him as he tries, unsuccessfully, to punt the football over his house. Even on his best kicks, even when he deliberately wears a heavy boot on his kicking foot, the boy can only send the ball to the roof, which sends it back to him, end over end, hard to catch.

Nice try! Alan says.

You almost had it! Chris says.

And then the two of them cheer like mad when the boy catches the ball off the roof without even bobbling it.

———

THE GIRL keeps a marching baton beneath her bed. The baton is capped at each end with a mushroom-shaped rubber stopper, to aid in balancing, the girl supposes, although it has been ages since she actually twirled the baton. A funny thing about the baton is that you can remove one of the rubber stoppers if you give it a few good twists—there! Inside, a dark hollow the approximate width of a garden hose. Within this space, the girl hides notes. Notes written on the "From the Desk Of" stationery her father has left behind. The girl likes stationery. She acquires more and more of it with each passing holiday and birthday. When her family thinks of what to get her, the girl realizes, they always think *stationery*.

One of the notes says, *When I am married, I will have three children named Finley, Madison, and Dexter.* Another note says, *If you are reading this note, you are a spy!* Another: *I bet you thought this note was going to have something secret, ha!* Another: *I don't really believe in God, unless you are reading this right now, God. Sorry, God!* There's one note that's been stuck inside the baton so long—it's jammed at the opposite end, just visible when the girl tilts the baton toward her desk lamp—that the girl cannot remember what it says anymore. The girl has tried to twist the stopper off at the end that holds the jammed note, but no luck. What does the note say? It must have been the first note the girl hid inside the baton, the girl thinks. Back before she'd mastered the rolling technique that allows the stationery to slide easily into the baton without slipping to the opposite end, out of reach.

If an intruder ever comes into their house, the girl plans to surprise the intruder with the marching baton. The girl imagines it, the moment the intruder realizes the girl has kept the baton beneath her bed for an occasion like this. The intruder's look of surprise when the girl brandishes the baton like a battle-axe. The intruder's recognition of the girl's secret strength, resourcefulness, and cunning, held, until this moment, in reserve.

I see, the intruder says.

————

ONE OF THE mother's friends wants to fix her up with a guy she knows. A nice guy, she says. Not bad looking. "Recently separated," she whispers, and makes a face meant to suggest that this might be a slightly embarrassing condition.

"You do realize I'm recently separated too, right?" the mother says.

The friend says she knows that, of course; that's why she thought this guy might be a good a candidate. "You'd have, you know, something in common."

"Right. Common damage."

"That's not what I meant!"

"A little bit," the mother says. "A little bit that's what you meant."

"I just thought he was a nice guy, that's all."

"Nice, plus recently separated."

"You're taking this the wrong way!"

The mother detects a gathering slickness in the friend's eyes. Oh, it's time to relent, the little voice in her head says, the way it sometimes does. "I'm sorry," she says. "I know you didn't mean it that way." There.

The friend says thank you and, sensing her sudden advantage, says, "I told him I thought you two should meet sometime."

"You didn't."

"I did!" The friend claps her hands together. "You know how I am."

"I know how you are."

"Well, guess what? He said he'd like to meet you sometime."

"No."

"Oh, stop it," the friend says. "Don't be like that."

"I don't want to meet him."

"But why not?"

The mother can think of so many reasons they crowd one another out. Hard to pick from so many. The mother settles on "no."

"His name is Cliff."

"Cliff? I don't want to meet someone named Cliff. No one has ever wanted to meet someone named Cliff. Ever."

The friend tells the mother she's being ridiculous but laughs anyway. She tells the mother to let her know if she changes her mind.

"Oh," the friend says, and this is the thing the mother will later think was the thing that changed her mind when, a few weeks later, she agrees to meet Cliff for lunch after all. "He has a son."

———

ANYONE COULD enter this house, the girl thinks, on a night when she's failing, yet again, to fall asleep. Don't think a locked door will stop them. That's laughable really. The front door is practically falling off its hinges now that their father has moved out, the father not around to make minor but necessary repairs, it's true. Just pull the knob and hear those hinges creak. The sliding glass doors to the back deck wear a pathetic little lock as firm and flimsy as a clutch purse's. The garage door doesn't even have a lock, as far as the girl can tell. What's to stop someone from breaking in? Nothing, that's what.

"Remember," Gumma said, the last time she called, "if someone really wants to get into your house, they will."

And the girl had thought of her baton and felt dumb and foolish and childish.

"Best bet is to run," Gumma said. "And, if there's nowhere to run, hide."

The girl imagines the space beneath her bed.

"And if there's nowhere to hide," Gumma says, "fight back."

————

SOMETIMES THE father tries to help the boy with his pronunciation. The boy has a hard time closing his mouth around certain words, the father informs him. He needs to close his mouth more often. After all, it's not like he's trying to be a ventriloquist, right?

"What's a ventriloquist?" the boy asks.

The father explains.

"Oh," the boy says. He knows what those are. Those are about the scariest things ever. Does his father think he's scary?

"Let's try this one," the father says. "'Mommy makes mushy meatballs.'"

"She does?"

"Not really. It's just an example."

"Oh."

"'Mommy makes mushy meatballs,'" the father says, emphasizing the first letter of each word in a way the boy would usually find funny if he wasn't so unsettled by his father's expression, a strange compound of hope, anxiety, and annoyance. They are sitting at his father's breakfast table, the one that faces the balcony overlooking the swimming pool. The boy's sister and Sarah are out on an errand somewhere, the way they are more and more often now, the two of them sometimes laughing at things the boy and the father have no idea about. "Women," the father will say, and shoot the boy a look. "What can you do?"

"I don't want to say it," the boy says.

"Oh, come on," the father says. "You can say it once, can't you? 'Mommy makes mushy meatballs.' See? Just try it one time."

The boy knows what he is supposed to do. He is supposed to say the words and make his lips come together the way his father wants him to. The boy's lips concern the father, the way they sometimes don't move at all, even when the boy is talking a mile a minute, as his mother would say. The boy knows that. But what the boy wants to tell his father is that he can make his lips come together the right way whenever he wants to; it's just that he can't always think about it the way his father does since the boy can't see his lips when he speaks, so it doesn't seem like a big deal really. But the boy must please his father, so he says, "Mommy. Makes. Mushy. Meatballs," the way he knows he must if he is to be understood when he grows up and goes out into the world.

His father aims an awkward smile at him. "Close," he says. "Better."

———

NO ONE FOLDS the laundry anymore, so the girl folds the laundry. It is amazing how much laundry there is to fold. The girl had no idea. Kind separation, only wishing to expand what the girl does not know to what the girl now knows. Turns out the family has more washcloths than the girl can count: the boy is the culprit; he still uses a washcloth in the tub, like a baby. The girl stacks these into the laundry basket between the hand towels and bath towels. Half the trick of folding is figuring out your stacking system, the girl is starting to learn. Build up from the bottom of the basket; save larger items for the top—secure these, in transit, with the bottom of your chin. Secured, the laundry gives off the smell of lavender.

The girl isn't sure at first whether to fold her mother's bras or not, but after they begin to collect atop the dryer, she places them in the basket as well. Tough to fold, bras. Same goes for blouses. The girl will not, under any circumstances, fold her brother's underwear. She lets it linger in the basket, where it gathers with all the other items she won't fold either, the idea of folding her mother's underwear an intimacy too embarrassing to bear. There really is no right way to fold a bottom bedsheet. If someone would like to show the girl how to fold a bottom bedsheet, well, that's not something the girl would be opposed to. Whose idea was it to gird the sheet with elastic anyway?

After the girl is finished folding, she carries the basket upstairs and leaves it at the top of the stairs, where, eventually, her mother will see it and put her clothes away. The basket, empty, depresses the girl, who is usually the one to return it to the laundry room unless her mother beats her to it.

One time, the girl is carrying the basket up the stairs, when she bumps into her mother heading the other way.

"You can stop doing that," the mother says, "from now on."

"I don't mind," the girl says.

"Well, you can stop anyway."

"OK."

"Because it feels like a criticism," the mother says.

The girl says it is not a criticism.

"A little bit it is," the mother says.

The girl says she didn't mean it that way.

"I know you want me to be some other kind of mother."

"No," the girl says.

"Someone different."

"No."

"One day, all your dreams will come true," the mother says, and then gives the girl a look she isn't sure how to read. "And then what will you do?"

———

ONE SUNDAY, the father tells the children he wants to go to mass with them. The children tell him he doesn't have to do that. Their father hasn't been to mass in years. Why would he want to go with them?

"Church is boring," the boy explains.

"Super boring," the girl says.

But their father doesn't say anything. Instead, he parks the car near the side entrance and reties the boy's oxfords before holding the door for a family with two babies, one asleep against the mother's shoulder, the other gumming a green plastic ring the size of a wristwatch. Babies' heads are so big, the girl thinks.

Inside, the father dips his finger in holy water and makes the sign of the cross before leading the children to the front pew. The children have never sat in the front pew and would point out that there are nearly a dozen open pews that are not the front pew if their father wasn't already seated in the front pew, now lowering the kneeler to the floor, now kneeling, now making the sign of the cross again, and now closing his eyes and steepling his prayerful hands in front of him in what seems to the girl both an act of devotion and a parody. His lips mouth words the children cannot hear. The boy gives the girl a look meant to ask, What should we do? The girl nudges the boy into the pew, where he makes the sign of the cross too and kneels in a fair approximation of their father. The girl kneels, sensing other families watching them. Who is this new family with a devout single dad among this congregation of women, children, and senior citizens?

The father can recite the creed without reading from the hymnal, the way the girl and boy must. The father bows his head at "and was born of the Virgin Mary and became man" the way only the older congregants do. When he receives the host, his "amen" is loud enough that the girl can hear it from where she stands in line, the girl old enough now to receive communion, unlike her brother, who must wait until next year. The girl watches her father drink from the cup, something she never does. She follows him back to their pew. The father kneels and prays, even when the rest of their row lifts the kneelers back in place.

Afterward, the father takes them to a car wash and permits them to spray the car with a threatening hose and soap the car's windows with a giant, foaming brush.

"Don't forget the roof," the father says.

The girl rises on tiptoe and brings the brush to the roof.

The timer beeps. They need more dimes. The father checks his pockets. "Here," he says, handing the boy twenty cents. When the dimes fall into the coin slot, the machine makes an approving noise.

SIX

IF THE GIRL takes any longer in the bathroom, her mother says she doesn't know what she's going to do. She's going to remove the lock from the door. She's going to remove the light bulbs from the ceiling fixture. She's going to start deducting TV time for all the time the girl spends in the bathroom, at an unfavorable markup. She's going to stand in the bathroom with the girl, just like when she was little. What could take her so long in the bathroom?

"I'm drying my hair," the girl says, which is sort of true.

"How could drying your hair take that long?"

The girl shrugs. Powerful move, the shrug. Try it, and you'll see.

"What are you smiling about?"

"Nothing. Sorry."

"Don't be sorry," the mother says. "Be quicker."

The truth is the girl likes to watch herself in the bathroom mirror. She likes the bathroom mirror, trimmed with bright bulbs, the girl a sudden actress preparing for opening night the moment she steps to the bathmat and brings her towel to the mirror, the towel describing a circle in the center, one that returns the girl looking at herself, hair slicked back, eyes difficult to read, expression noncommittal. Is this the way she looks to other people? Or is it the way she looks a few moments later, the mirror's fog losing its grip? The girl leans closer, deciding.

The mirror clears.

Her mother knocks at the door.

SOMETIMES THE boy thinks terrible thoughts. Like the way everyone he knows will die, eventually, the way they certainly will, like everyone he meets or sees passing by or sees in a magazine or watches on TV, which is almost too much to think about, so the boy does not think about it. Then he feels fine for a while, a long time really—it is amazing all the things you can avoid thinking about for a long time—until he starts thinking about it again.

One night, the boy cannot sleep. One day, he knows, he too will die. He tries to imagine being dead, but his imagination only summons a cartoon cliff fitted out with a single, flimsy branch, from which the boy hopelessly hangs, like Wile E. Coyote, the moment before the branch breaks and sends the boy plummeting to his death, a plume of dust rising from the desert floor. The boy places his hands beneath his pillow, seeks out the coolness there.

ONE AFTERNOON while the girl is standing on her father's balcony, trying to decide whether they have time to get in a swim before it rains, she sees the bicycle man again. He's touring the parking lot at a crawl, his legs barely turning the pedals. He's got sunglasses on today, the wraparound kind, too big for his face, and unnecessary at the moment: the sun is nowhere to be found. Fat clouds cast the parking lot into shadow. For a moment, the girl feels superior to the bicycle man, spying on him while he has no idea, but then she wonders what would happen if he looked up and saw her standing there on her father's balcony. Would he be able to see her? Would he be able to figure out which apartment she lives in? Would he count the balconies, guess which door was hers, and show up on their doorstep sometime when her father is away?

"What's gotten into you?" her father asks, when the girl pushes the balcony's screen door open, steps inside, and closes it more sharply than she intended.

"Rain," she says.

———

THE NEXT TIME the babysitter babysits the children, he tells them a friend of his will be stopping by later. He hopes that's OK, because he wouldn't like to do anything that might get him in trouble. Like if their mom found out? How that would be detrimental to his babysitting income? In light of how he's trying to acquire more money, not the opposite, which would be losing money? Because of his car and because of life, which makes you need money all the time? That's something the children will figure out soon, he tells them. Everything costs money. *Everything.*

"Hey," he says. "Do you guys still have that weird bank?"

The children tell him yes.

"How much is in there now?"

The boy tells him.

"That's it? Man, that sucks."

The boy tells him he hasn't really been paying attention to it.

"Well, you should," the babysitter says. "Save your pennies."

"You can't put pennies into it," the girl says.

"No, that's like a famous saying," the babysitter explains. "Haven't you ever heard that?"

"No," the girl says.

"Save your pennies," the babysitter intones, "or else you have to earn them."

"It's for dimes and stuff," the boy says.

"Go get it," the babysitter says.

"Don't get it," the girl says.

But the boy runs upstairs to retrieve the bank anyway, his

heart beating in his ears. When he returns, the babysitter has already fished two nickels out of his pockets and placed them on the kitchen table, an offering. The boy sets the bank on the table, which has been hastily swept of all the bills, catalogs, letters, grocery bags, and coupons that have been there for weeks now, the table no longer a table, more like an open junk drawer their mother keeps promising to get around to. For nearly two months now a fat jar of horseradish has kept a stack of newspapers from fleeing the table, the stack mysteriously acquiring two boxes of paperclips, a single 9-volt battery, a booklet of stamps, a bag of blue and green rubber bands, and a black umbrella still encased in its plastic sleeve.

"OK," the babysitter says, dropping one nickel into the slot. "You're going to need this one day. Trust me." He pulls the lever; the bank swallows the nickel. "One day you'll get this nickel back and be like, Hey, I remember that nickel!" The babysitter shows them the next nickel, which, the babysitter explains, he has inked with a red marker, so they'll remember it. "See? Cool, right?"

The children agree that the red nickel is cool. The babysitter tells them they can drop it in the slot, and the boy obliges, the nickel cool to the touch and vaguely misshapen. The bank accepts it anyway. The boy reads the new total, which fails to console him: it's going to take weeks to hit ten dollars. Months.

Later, the babysitter's friend arrives. A not-very-pretty girl in acid wash jeans and a concert T-shirt, hair tied back with a headscarf, ears sporting earrings shaped like feathers. The friend's outfit is more like a costume than clothes the girl thinks, but then feels guilty for thinking that. She's got to stop thinking things like that, she really does. All those uncharitable thoughts crowding one another out, one after the other—will there be enough room for them all? Yes, a glance at the friend's toenails informs her, each nail painted sparkly pink. Yes, there's always room for more.

After the children have pretended to brush their teeth and donned the same sleep clothes they've been wearing for the past week, the four of them watch TV together in the family room. The children sit at the foot of the sofa. The babysitter and his friend sit on the sofa, talking beneath the show, a sitcom the children do not understand, unlike the studio audience, who applaud whenever a new character appears. TV is really sort of terrible, the boy realizes, just like everyone says it is, even if watching TV is about the only time he feels he's truly safe, truly normal, truly at home. Another secret the boy is glad to keep.

After a while, the babysitter's friend says, "Have you two ever seen a boy kiss a girl?"

The children look up at them. The babysitter's friend is lying across the babysitter's lap, her face inches from his.

"Sure," the girl says. "Everybody has."

The boy, who cannot recall seeing that, nods in agreement.

"I mean for real," the babysitter's friend says. "For *real*, kiss a girl."

"I guess," the girl says.

"I think so," the boy says.

"If you ever saw a boy kiss a girl for real, you would know so," the friend says, and then she does something the children will remember forever, although the two of them will never talk about it, the memory as clear and bright and yet invisible as the night their parents called them up the stairs and did not punish them after all for Smash Up Derby.

The friend closes her eyes and sticks out her tongue. The babysitter does the same, their tongues not touching, missing one another, until the friend raises her head and the two of them meet for real.

HE'S GOT TO be kidding about those corduroys, the mother thinks the next time the father picks the children up for the weekend. How many times did she try to get him to wear corduroys? His objection: he didn't like the faint swishing sound they made. Made him feel too self-conscious. Well, he's not feeling too self-conscious now, is he?

———

A TRIP TO their father's office on a weekend afternoon: a chore, a thing to be resented, worthy of complaint. Why do we have to go to your office on a Saturday? Why can't we stay at the apartment by ourselves until you get back? Please can we stay at the apartment until you get back? Mom would let us!

The father tells them he only has to pick up a few papers; they won't be there long. Just a few minutes.

But the office is so boring, the children complain.

They are pulling into the office parking lot. The father has the car windows down, his eyes masked by sunglasses, something new for him, another Sarah novelty to go along with leather sandals, rock cassettes, and wheat germ. The father slows the car into a parking space, rolls the windows up, and says, "Well, some things are boring."

Inside, the office is dark. The father switches the lights on, an irregular sky of fluorescent tubes and ceiling tiles. The children fill paper cones from the water cooler, an inverted jug that sends a threatening bubble to the surface. They drink their water in two long swallows, the water so cold it hurts their teeth.

"Ah," the boy says.

"Ah," the girl agrees.

The father sits at his desk and types a letter. The typewriter hums and sings. Their father is a remarkable typist, the children know, from the many times they've seen him poised before his IBM Selectric, his hands moving across the keys, which mysteriously instruct a metallic ball to march across the blank page and transform it into a letter. He finishes one letter and then begins another. "Just two more to go," he says. "Then we're out of here."

The boy sits at the desk he's permitted to use during office visits and removes a plastic cover from another IBM Selectric, this one orange, an incorrect color for a typewriter, but one that has the effect of enlisting the boy's sympathy for it nonetheless. Poor orange typewriter, the boy thinks. No one even minds if a kid uses you. The boy turns the typewriter on, a satisfying click that yields to the typewriter's ambient noise. The boy scrolls a piece of paper into the carriage but has no idea what to write. He could write a letter, like his dad, but to whom?

The girl reminds her father he said he only had to pick up a few papers, but he doesn't say anything, the way he usually does when he's typing, the way he used to when he lived in the house with them, working late into the night sometimes in his basement office, the door partially closed, but wide enough to admit the girl, who only wanted to remind her father that he'd promised to kiss her goodnight. On those nights, the girl would wait until her father detected her presence, the fog of typewriter noise lifting the moment he removed the paper from the carriage and turned to see her in the doorway. "I didn't forget," her father would say, as if to reassure her, and the girl would say, "I know." It occurs to the girl now, that ritual has become a memory. Forget it and it's gone.

"Dad," the girl says.

The boy types a sentence. *How are you?* And then another: *I am fine.*

THE COUNTRY keeps on drying up. Thirsty America, barely able to clear its dusty throat. Gas lines grow longer; see them snaking from the gas station's intersection to the supermarket parking lot, where, the mother tells the children, they have no choice but to wait it out. Again. The girl sighs, says she's not going to wait with them; she's going to walk home. It's less than a mile, after all. She can walk a mile, can't she? The boy says if the girl gets to walk home, then he should get to walk home too. The girl says there's no way she's letting him walk home with her, but the boy says she is not, in fact, the boss of him. The girl says he might want to check the facts on that one. The boy says it isn't fair if she gets to walk home and he doesn't. The girl says life isn't fair. Is too, the boy says.

"Quiet, you two," the mother warns. "Nobody is walking home."

"Well, I am," the girl says, and dares to unlock her door, a move the mother anticipates without even a glance in the rearview mirror.

"Try that again," the mother says, locking the doors with the push of a single button, "and you're not going to your father's this weekend."

"Oh, real nice," the girl says. "That's really great. What a great way to treat a child."

"Careful," the mother says.

The girl wants to put her away, but she isn't sure what the next move is really. The next move turns its palms up to her, says, I dunno? So the girl compromises: she sticks her face out the window, as if to say I am not here. I am outside, where you people are not. And there's nothing you can do about it. Which is a pretty good move, the girl thinks, until their car inches closer to the gas station, where the girl can now see a blue sedan blocking a white pickup truck from the station's entrance. The white pickup is trying to nose ahead of the sedan; the pickup driver sounds the horn, a sustained signal that gets everyone's attention, but not the sedan driver, who, the girl can see, isn't looking back. The truck honks again, moves closer. The sedan rolls forward, ignoring the truck.

And then the girl sees something she will not forget, something her mother and brother must witness too, although they never discuss it later. The pickup driver gets out of his car, approaches the sedan, knocks his hands against the driver's side window. "Hey asshole!" the pickup truck driver shouts. "Hey asshole, come on out!" The sedan driver rolls his window halfway down, not enough for the girl to see his face, but enough for the pickup driver to bring his fists down on the window, hard, and smash it to smithereens. Glass goes everywhere, glittering, catching the sun.

New sign outside the station: GAS SHORTAGE IS GOING TO GET THE WORLD BACK ON ITS FEET.

———

CLIFF TAKES the mother out for lunch. A kind man, the mother will later say, when her friend asks her what he's like. And she will mean it. Cliff is a kind man, a dull dresser, a solicitous listener, a wearer of unfashionable glasses, a good laugher, a drinker of unsweetened iced tea, a brown-not-black wallet bearer.

"I'll get it," the mother says, when Cliff produces his credit card from the wallet.

"Please," Cliff says. "It's nothing."

"Well, OK," the mother says. "Thank you."

"I'm supposed to say, 'No, thank you,'" Cliff laughs.

The mother smiles.

"It was nice getting to meet you today," Cliff says.

"Yes," the mother says, so neutrally she's afraid she's hurt Cliff's feelings, but Cliff doesn't seem to notice or does an excellent job pretending he doesn't. Oh, these first steps of getting to know someone, the mother thinks. A distant little dance whose moves feel as strange as a box step to her now.

"I know Marcus would love to meet your kids someday," Cliff says. Marcus, Cliff's twelve-year-old son, as the mother has recently learned, a kid shuttled between his mother and father, like her own but at greater distances. Marcus's mother has custody of him in Texas. But Marcus spends part of his summer here in Delaware. He'll be here next week, Cliff volunteers, chancing a look at the mother, who knows she should say, We should get them together, but only nods and says, That's wonderful. *That's wonderful!* But what else can she say? That's what the mother would like to know; what else can she say?

Cliff nods and signs the check. Tucks the pen inside the ledger. "We usually go canoeing," he says. "Or paddleboating. Do you ever take your kids out to Lums Pond?"

The mother recalls their one and only trip to Lums Pond, last summer, her marriage just starting to turn. She and the children rented a canoe already two inches deep with pond water, the children afraid to put their feet down, afraid the canoe would sink, no matter how many times the mother told them they were fine, even though it did seem like the canoe was sinking, especially the stern, where the mother sat uncomfortably on a damp seat and accidentally steered them into a felled tree. The tree clutched them for nearly ten minutes while the mother assuaged the children with the snack cakes she'd hidden inside her purse, but then her purse fell into the canoe water and she'd said, "Fuck," and the children stopped eating their cakes.

"We love Lums Pond," the mother says.

"That's good," Cliff says, as if something has been agreed on. "That's great."

SOMETIMES THE girl gets mad for no reason. The girl will get mad at her mother, or she'll get angry with her brother. God, can she get angry with her brother. Sometimes just the sight of him watching TV with his dopey brother face all slack and spacey, or chewing his food the way he does, his mouth agape, his fingers slick with pizza grease, is enough to set her off. It's like the girl feels a little mad about something all the time now.

Take tonight, for example. The three of them eat dinner in front of the TV, like always, the girl's mother seated at the far end of the blue sofa, like always, the boy sitting cross-legged on the floor with his plate balanced atop his knees, like always, and the girl seated at the opposite end of the sofa, her plate on her lap, a squat glass of Coke perched on the armrest, like always. Dinner in front of the TV, a ritual the girl usually looks forward to, a routine to place alongside getting donuts and a newspaper after church or reading one page of a Nancy Drew mystery before she turns off her bedroom light and places her hands beneath the pillow. But something is off tonight. The sight of her mother using her fork and knife to cut a chicken breast infuriates her. Her brother's balanced plate, an annoyance, as irritating as the sitcom they are watching. Everyone has it right: television is a waste of time. The boob tube. The idiot box. Why must they always eat dinner in front of the TV?

The girl stands and carries her plate to the kitchen. She would sit down at the kitchen table and finish her dinner, but the table is covered with papers, so many papers, including the ones the girl has already stacked into orderly piles, the piles subsumed by subsequent layers of papers, that she cannot even imagine moving the piles to the countertop to accommodate her plate. Solution? The girl rests the plate on the countertop and eats her meal while watching her mother and brother not noticing her watching them eat dinner in front of the TV. Rinses her plate in a hurry. Lets the silverware clang into the sink. Ignores the spoon that falls into the drain and will likely get mauled by the disposal. Never mind the spoon. The girl has some serious stomping to do on the way upstairs to her bedroom.

"Something the matter?" her mom calls out to her.

But the girl is too sharp to fall for that. Respond and you might as well say, "No, I'm only trying to call childish attention to myself and my childish anger." Ha! The girl is a better player than that. That's why she slams her bedroom door—whoomp!—and throws herself across her bed, to make a point about what a superior player she is.

And, as if to best the girl's challenge, her mother doesn't even follow her upstairs.

———

ANOTHER THING about your parents splitting up and living in separate places is having *two* bedrooms. His whole life, the boy thought he was a one-bedroom kind of boy, but it turns out he was mistaken; he's very much a two-bedroom boy, this separation is starting to let him know. For starters, two bedrooms means *two* beds, and two beds means you get to pick one of them, as the boy did for his apartment bedroom. The boy chose a full-size mattress, which he didn't even know was a thing but turns out is definitely a thing. Full-size means the boy can stretch his body into an X, with his arms at each corner and his legs nearly but not quite touching the foot of the bed, something that's nearly impossible to do at his mother's house on his twin-size mattress. But his twin-size bed is easier to make since it can be centered in the middle of the room, unlike the full-size bed, which must go in the corner to make room for the boy's dresser and nightstand. Making the full-size bed is a chore, especially the part where the boy must reach across the mattress and tuck the comforter between the mattress and wall. Problem: impossible to smooth the comforter into compliance. Problem: one end always hangs down lower than the other, uneven, maddening. Solution: don't make your bed!

Although he cannot prove it, and although no one will ever ask him to do so, the boy believes he has different kinds of dreams in different beds. Twin-size dreams and full-size dreams. Twin-size dreams are endings without beginnings or middles. In his twin-size dreams, the boy is suddenly made to understand something — he has forgotten to wear clothes to school again, a celebrity is honored to know him, werewolves disappear from view whenever the boy opens the basement door — and then the dream concludes, easily forgotten. Full-size dreams, though, greet the boy halfway through, a movie the boy has wandered into late, the show already in gear by the time the boy arrives, too late to grasp what's going on, but trying nonetheless. Like: his aunt is angry with him for something he did, even though the boy knows it was not his fault; if he could only explain himself, she would understand. Or: the boy has bicycled to a place he should not have bicycled to, but if he turns around now, he still has a chance of making it back home before anyone notices. Or: the boy is watching an event from a great distance and gradually comes to understand that the event is happening for his benefit and so feels comfortable pushing through the crowd to obtain a closer view.

But the strangest part of having two bedrooms? Waking up and wondering, for a moment, which room you're in.

————

ONE NIGHT, the girl liberates the stuck note from the baton. The note falls to her bed, where she's piled the other notes, rereading them late at night while her mother and brother sleep and the only sound in the house is her brother's fan, turning on its base.

The girl picks up the note and reads it. *Hi,* the note begins, in the girl's three-years-ago script, embarrassing to her now. *If you find this baton, please bring it back! Don't be a stealer!!* The girl has signed the note and drawn a puppy, heart, rainbow, and happy face at the bottom. The happy face is wearing glasses.

The girl reads the note again to see if it is as embarrassing as she thinks it is. Yes, the exclamation marks say. Absolutely, the puppy agrees.

The girl folds the note up, drops it into the baton along with all the other notes, and shoves the baton back underneath her bed. She will forget about the note. She will forget about the baton. Just like she forgot writing the note and drawing those drawings way back when. Way back when. She will leave the baton in the way back when. Along with embarrassment. Shame. Bespectacled happy faces. You can leave whatever you want in the way back when, and there's nothing anyone can do about it.

"What's so funny?" her mother says to her, the next morning at breakfast.

The girl shrugs. Pours orange juice into a small glass. "Nothing."

"Just feeling chipper today?"

"What's chipper?" the boy asks.

"Chipper means happy," the mother says.

"Oh," the boy says. Then, "That's dumb."

SEVEN

A NEW THING: Sarah takes the children to the pool without their father. Their father is busy, he says; he has some work to catch up on. They should go ahead without him. No need to waste a sunny Saturday on his account. Get some fresh air! Enjoy the pool. Maybe he'll stop by and check on them in a little while if he gets enough work done.

"You have half an hour," Sarah tells him.

"Well, I'm not sure I'll be able to —"

"Twenty-nine minutes," Sarah says, "and counting."

Another new thing: the two of them argue. A quiet argument that doesn't seem like an argument at first, the girl thinks, but is definitely an argument. When they argue, Sarah lowers her voice and gestures with her hands, while the father grows silent, sullen; the argument usually ends with him walking away from Sarah or pretending to read something while she's still standing there, as if to say, I see that you are still there arguing with me, but I will have nothing to do with it. The girl understands that move; she uses that one on her mother sometimes, often with excellent results. The girl has turned a lost cause into a near victory with that move.

The pool is crowded today. Mothers tan themselves on long chairs draped with towels, their children's arms cartoonishly muscled with inflatable floats. Fathers tread deep-end water, their bald spots gleaming, as they hoist children onto their reddening shoulders, the children shouting, "Throw me again!" Sarah guides them to a chair and reminds them they still need suntan lotion, something the children would normally protest against, but not today, not after witnessing Sarah put their father in his place. So they close their eyes when Sarah tells them to close their eyes and turn their noses to the sun while Sarah works the lotion beneath their chins. Eyes closed, the pool seems a menacing place, a series of shouts, screams, and exclamations punctuated by cannonballs. With eyes open, the pool is fun, silly even, a joke everyone agrees isn't funny but laughs at anyway.

The boy has a fear of jumping straight into the pool the way his sister and Sarah do. The boy cannot imagine doing that. Instead, the boy likes to test the water by the shallow-end stairs, taking his time, one step and the next, the pool waves threatening to splash his bathing suit. The boy's sister makes fun of him, the way he stands on the shallow-end stairs with his arms tremblingly raised like a breezed scarecrow. "Just jump in, scaredy-cat!" she says. Scaredy-cat, the boy thinks. The last time he saw the family cat, it was hiding beneath his mother's car. Ran the moment he crouched down and whispered its name. But the boy knew the cat was only acting on instinct and didn't want him to take it personally. The thing is, the cat missed him terribly but didn't know quite how to express it. "I know," the boy said, to the benefit of the cat's retreating body.

The girl stands on the diving board and raises her arms above her head. She's not a great swimmer, but she knows enough to know you don't enter the pool the way her brother does. What her brother doesn't get that she gets is that everyone is looking at you all the time, everywhere you go, news the girl has been catching on to more and more lately. Like right now, she can see Sarah removing her cover-up and folding it into a pillow, which is what anyone would see, of course, if they were looking at Sarah, but what the girl also sees is that the father playing with his kids near the shallow end is actually watching Sarah take her cover-up off and fold it into a pillow. Because whenever they go to the pool, men look at Sarah. Something the girl has clued in to and something her brother has no idea about. See him flinch when a kid in a snorkel splashes nearby. The girl watches her dumb little brother and feels a sudden anger toward him. To chase it away, the girl dives into the pool. When she surfaces, her brother is standing on tiptoe in the shallow end, arms outstretched, afraid.

The girl treads water, shakes her head. A secret: the girl likes the feeling of water in her ears, at least for the first few seconds, the outside world held momentarily at bay, so that the inner one might roam about. Is that the world where her thoughts play like a movie on a screen? Or is the inside more like the school gymnasium after a game has ended and no one is there, and your shoes make sounds like kisses? She swims to the center of the pool, where her brother is clinging to the shallow-end rope.

"You're not supposed to hang on the rope," she reminds him.

Her brother, affecting indifference, says, "Is there any law against hanging on the rope?" This, a line he must have overheard from Alan and Chris, the two neighborhood boys who come over to the house from time to time and kick footballs over the house, her brother retrieving them like a dumb puppy. Another secret: sometimes the boys give her looks like the ones the fathers give Sarah at the pool, something the girl would never tell anyone, ever, and something she isn't quite sure how to feel about, except that whenever the boys come over to kick the football, the girl makes a point to walk outside and tell her brother to come inside, not because she really wants him to come inside, but because she wants to see if the boys will look at her that way. Whenever she catches them looking, the boys immediately look away like they weren't looking at all, and the girl feels both proud and embarrassed, adored and violated, and isn't the world a strange place?

The girl plays with her brother for a while until Sarah calls for her. When the girl arrives, Sarah tells her to go get her father. "Tell him we need him to pry your brother off the ropes," Sarah says. "Tell him he won't let go." The girl laughs, but when she wraps a towel around her waist and urges her wet feet inside her flip-flops, she feels a sudden unease. Will her father be angry? What if he says he's not coming after all? The girl enters the apartment hallway with the feeling that she's been sent to the principal's office for an offense she doesn't even know.

Inside, the apartment is dark, the shades drawn. "Dad?" the girl says. It is freezing; the girl is still wet from swimming, her skin gooseflesh. Her father is sitting on the sofa, eyes closed, with headphones on. A record spins on the turntable; the girl can see the needle is nearing the end. The girl knows what will happen next: the needle will rise from the record and her father will open his eyes and see her watching him when he thought he was alone, and he will have to say hi and act pleased to find her standing there, but really he will feel exposed, embarrassed. But the girl is not going to let that happen. No. She backs out of the room as quietly as possible, opens the door without making a sound — the girl is good at things like this, even if no one knows it — and closes the door before the record ends. Her father will never know she was there. A comforting idea, the girl believes, until she reaches the pool and Sarah gives her a look.

"Have you been crying?" Sarah asks.

"No," the girl says.

"Are you sure?"

The girl nods.

"Is everything OK?"

The girl says everything's fine, but when Sarah doesn't ask about her father, about why she didn't return with him, the girl knows Sarah is letting her off easy.

THE MOTHER goes on another date with Cliff, she supposes, although it doesn't exactly feel like a date. More like an outing. Or a not terribly interesting conversation interrupted by a movie. Or a declined kiss prefaced by a silent ride home. Or, at least, that's how she tries to explain it to her friend later on the phone, when her friend asks, Well, how's it going with Cliff?

"Guarded," the mother says.

"Guarded?"

"Yes, I think so."

"What are you being guarded about?"

"About everything, what else?"

The friend says, "Jokes. All you want to do is make jokes."

The mother says, "But what if jokes are all I have?"

"You need to let him know whether you're interested in him or not. It's cruel to lead him on if you can't even make up your mind about how you feel."

"Are you serious?" the mother says. "We've only been on two dates. Since when did those rules come into play?"

"Since you were off being married," the friend says.

"*Off being married*," the mother says. "Maybe I should write that with shaving cream on my car window."

"Jokes."

"Cliff would probably say how nice it looks."

"Fine, Cliff is dull," the friend says. "Cliff is boring. Cliff is a snore. So tell him you're not interested and get it over with."

The mother recalls Cliff's expression the moment she pulled away from his kiss. He didn't look disappointed so much as relieved that she played it off as if it hadn't happened at all; she did that sometimes too. "He's not boring," the mother says. "Well, no, he is sort of boring, but harmless, earnest. Earnest but harmless. Plus nice."

"Such high praise," the friend says.

"We should all be so lucky," the mother says.

But the mother knows the reason she's guarded around Cliff: because Cliff often injects Marcus into their conversations, wanting, the mother knows, for her to say that Marcus should get together with her kids soon.

"Not ready yet," the mother says.

"Ready for what?" the friend asks, but the mother steers the conversation away before the friend realizes the mother forgot she was still talking to her.

———

FOR THE FIRST time in his life, the father must keep his car parked outside. An unforeseen consequence of separation: you might be separated from your garage too. No matter, the father thinks, even though he must roll his windows down and run the air conditioner on full blast each morning before pulling out of the apartment parking lot. How quickly he had forgotten about bachelorhood. The only meals he knows how to prepare are eggs, pancakes, waffles, oatmeal and, strangely, the best split pea soup he's ever tasted, even though the children won't touch the stuff. At the supermarket, he loads up on frozen pizza and yogurt, the food of the lonely. The father has little interest in cooking. The father has little interest in trying to replicate his ex's meals, tasty as they were. Since the separation, the father has felt increasingly not interested in things he's not interested in. If Sarah leads him to new water, though, who is he to say he won't take a sip, every now and then?

This afternoon, the father must go to the store. Milk. Plus kitchen trash bags. Plus some other essential he's utterly failing to recall. Why can't he seem to remember to write things down, as Sarah always does? Outside, it's hot; the parking lot asphalt faintly bakes in the sun. The father reaches his car, turns his key in the lock. When he opens the door, a cat shoots out from beneath and scampers toward the bushes lining the pool privacy fence. The father turns. Glimpses the cat the moment before the cat disappears from view. It is their old cat, the father thinks, but of course it is not. Not possible, or at least highly unlikely. The father climbs into his car, starts the engine, rolls down the windows, and runs the air conditioner.

Half and half, the father remembers. That was the other thing.

———

THE CHILDREN have an allowance now. Something new, to go along with two bedrooms, two homes, Sarah, babysitters, fixing their own lunches, separation, not mentioning the other parent when spending time with the other parent, lawn mowing, their mother's tears, the vanished cat, not mentioning Sarah around their mother, Magic Shell, skipping mass, seeing movies twice, and eating dinner in front of the television. The children get fifty cents for cleaning the upstairs bathroom—the *kids' bathroom*, as they call it—plus extra money for vacuuming, dusting, and sweeping. Unloading the dishwasher pays a measly twenty-five cents, but the boy prefers unloading to washing dishes by hand, also twenty-five cents, which doesn't seem fair since it takes forever to rid a Pyrex dish of a cheesy casserole, no matter how long you presoak the dish or how much dishwashing soap you squirt into its center. Dusting earns a walloping ten cents. Ten cents! The children protest, but their mother won't budge.

So, to the bathroom the boy goes, a heavy bucket of cleaning products in his impoverished hand. The boy starts with the toilet, the worst, most terrible job in the world. How can people stand this? the boy wonders, then remembers the money. To clean a toilet, you have to have a plan, the boy has discovered, and the boy's plan is to use as many paper towels as possible. If I'm not touching anything, then nothing is touching me, the boy thinks. Advanced technique: stand in front of the toilet like a center about to snap the football and work the paper towels beneath your feet so that your face keeps pleasantly away from the transaction. Only a rookie kneels before the toilet, as the boy did his first few times. Half the battle of cleaning the bathroom is figuring out where to *look*.

The boy cannot stand removing the clump of hair that forms in the shower drain, but fold three paper towels into one and sing as you close the towels together around the hair, and it's really little different than working the towels around the sink basin, the pleasing way the sink reveals another layer of gleam with each damp pass.

The bathroom mirror, a joy by comparison, the feeling of working the paper towels into whorls that widen and widen while the mirror squeaks and shows the boy back to himself in increasing clarity, his expression set, determined, the towel just starting to tear the moment the boy finishes and imagines someone admiring the mirror later, a bathroom visitor whose only thought is, What a clean mirror.

If you don't think about cleaning the space behind the toilet, it's like you aren't really cleaning the space behind the toilet.

Afterward, the bathroom exudes the smell of pine, ammonia, lemon.

Afterward, the boy cannot wash his hands enough.

Sometimes his mother forgets to give him the money, and the boy gets tired of asking her for it, and pretty soon he's cleaning the bathroom for free. The coin bank marks time at $4.75. The boy wishes he'd never put money in the bank. Why does everyone say you should put your money in the bank when putting money in the bank is like having no money at all? That's what the boy would like to know.

The girl keeps her money in a shoebox marked POSTCARDS. A secret. The girl has so many of them, and nobody even knows.

———

ONE NIGHT, Gumma calls again. The girl hands the phone to the boy, says, "Here, you talk to her," without saying a word to her.

The boy wears the dumb, dopey face he always gets when the girl tricks him into doing something he doesn't want to do. The little moron. Doesn't even know he can say no to things.

"Hello?" the boy says. Then, after a few moments of scrunching his sad, clueless face into an even more clueless one, he asks, "What's a 'momma's boy'?"

———

THE NEXT TIME Alan and Chris stop by, they keep asking the boy silly questions. "Me and Chris were thinking about having a party," Alan says. "Right, Chris?"

"Right," Chris says, and then laughs like Alan said something funny, which he didn't, not as far as the boy can tell. Alan and Chris are standing in the boy's driveway, tossing the boy's football high into the air and catching it themselves — they don't want the boy to hurt himself trying to catch these tosses, they tell him. He'd better keep his distance for now, for his own good, for his safety.

"And we were wondering if you could help us," Alan continues.

The boys says sure thing, he'd be glad to.

"Cool," Alan says, "that's cool of you."

But Chris is already giving Alan looks and then laughing noiselessly the way he sometimes does. The boy thinks this must be a signal that he should be laughing too, but he's never been good at that, fake laughter. The boy's experience has been that there are two kinds of people in the world: those who are good at fake laughter and him. So the boy does what he always does whenever he fails to laugh, which is nod his head for no apparent reason and smile like an idiot.

"Well, what me and Chris were wondering is, how much Coke should we get for our party?"

At this, Chris drops the football, hugs his arms to his chest, and laughs.

"Oh," the boy says. "Hm. I guess it depends on how many people are coming."

"Oh, everyone is going to want to come to this party," Alan says. "And everyone is going to want lots of Coke, that's for sure."

Chris's face is red with laughter. He falls to the ground and says, "Stop it, man. I'm going to pee my pants."

"It's pretty much a Coke party," Alan says. "So how much Coke do you think we'll need?"

The boy says, "I don't know, maybe five bottles?"

"Five bottles!" Chris says. "Oh, my God, stop!"

But Alan only nods as if he's taking the boy's counsel. "Five bottles, huh? Five bottles would probably be enough Coke, maybe under normal circumstances, but these people really, really like Coke, right Chris? It's like, they just can't get enough Coke."

"I'm dying," Chris laughs, and rolls to his side. "Please!"

"Well, I guess maybe you could get more Coke," the boy says, and then Chris starts kicking his legs like a half-squashed bug and pounding the ground with his skinny fists.

"More Coke, huh?" Alan says. "I guess that's right. We could get more Coke. But where would we get more Coke from?"

Chris grabs fistfuls of grass and cries, "I can't take it!"

The boy looks at Alan and feels as if he and Alan are working on something together, some project whose directions he's never seen but whose object is clear, to make Chris laugh. The boy brightens, says, "Oh, that's easy. You can get Coke just about any place."

Chris throws pulled grass into the air. "Oh, you can get it just about any place!"

"Yeah," the boy says, and, sensing his advantage, says, "Coke is everywhere."

Chris screams and kicks his legs. "He said Coke is everywhere!" he says, and then keeps saying it, over and over again. "Coke is everywhere! Ha! Coke is everywhere!"

All in all, the boy thinks, a pretty good day.

———

THE MOTHER must take exams. She buys blue books at the campus bookstore, stands in line with students nearly half her age. The mother did not go to college for a variety of reasons, but she isn't sure whether she regrets her decision or not. Not, she thinks, whenever she must find parking on campus, late from work, the children back home with the babysitter. Regret, whenever she visits the college library stacks, the fact of so many books in the world reminding her how little she will ever truly know. Sometimes the mother pulls a book from the shelf, just because, and reads the first few pages. So much labor has gone into these words, these paragraphs, these volumes. An abundance the mother has no idea what to do with. She returns the book to the shelf with the feeling of closing a heavy door.

Two girls—*women*, the mother reminds herself—wait in front of her, talking. The mother listens, but there's not much in their conversation to grab onto. One is telling the other one about her annoying roommate. The other girl listens, nods, says right, right, all while flipping through the college newspaper. The newspaper girl is pretty, the mother thinks, and wants to tell her so, but of course that's ridiculous. She isn't going to do that. She's just going to pay for her blue books and head off to class, where she is late again and must take a seat at the front of the room.

––––––––

GAS PRICES are going up. Ask anyone. A dollar per gallon. A dollar! It's getting so bad that people can't afford to drive to work. What are people supposed to do? That's what people always ask, the boy notices, whenever the local news reporter thrusts a bulbous microphone into their exasperated faces, just what are they supposed to *do*? People have jobs, after all. That's how they make money to pay the bills. If the bills don't get paid, then what? That's another thing the people on the news want to know: then what? And if there's no gas, there's no car, and if there's no car, there's no job, and if there's no job, then there's no food on the table. What are people supposed to do to put food on the table? The world's questions; there are so many more of them than answers. Finally, the boy thinks, something that won't run out.

––––––––

A SECRET: the father hates having to call the children on the phone. The way his voice gets, full of false cheer. He's no good at that. He's no phone father, this father. So little experience really. Bring on the weekend, the father thinks, when they can all go to the pool together or the movies.

––––––––

SARAH IS THE only one who understands the girl's hair. That's what the girl would like to tell her mother on those mornings when her mother instructs her to brush her hair again, even though, as the girl exasperatedly explains, she's already brushed it twice.

"Twice?" her mother laughs. "I think you missed. Both times."

The girl stomps upstairs, slams her bedroom door.

"We don't slam doors in this house!" her mother calls up the stairs.

"I do," the girl says, into her pillow. Oh, how the girl would love to say, "Sarah knows how to do a real French braid" or "Sarah says you shouldn't brush wet hair" or "Sarah has a special comb that gets all the knots out without even hurting." But the girl could never say that, of course, because the girl never says Sarah's name around her mother, ever. What the girl does instead is imagine she's explaining to Sarah how ridiculous her mom is being, as if Sarah were there, watching, observing, ready to listen, but not always to agree.

"She always does this," the girl imagines telling Sarah.

Sarah shrugs, says, "Tough job, being a mom."

"When I'm a mom, I'm going to let my daughter do whatever she wants to with her hair."

Sarah laughs. "You say that now."

"It's true! I swear to God I will."

"Maybe," Sarah says. "But one thing is for sure."

"What?"

"You either will or you won't."

"Argh!" The girl presses her face deep into the pillow. It's OK there, deep in the pillow. She closes her eyes, watches the movie that forever plays behind closed lids, a sort of *Fantasia*-incoherent-swirls-and-shapes thingy, minus the Bach. She could watch that film for a while, just here deep in the pillow, she could. Don't put it past her.

"What are you doing?" her mother says, her mother having materialized in the doorway while the girl was wherever. "Get your head off that pillow and go brush your hair like I told you to."

So the girl brushes her hair in the bathroom mirror, which apprises her that the pillow has made tiny indentations on her forehead.

ONE NIGHT, the boy hears another car crash. He wakes to find his fan tipped on its side, its oscillating head oscillating into his desk chair. A sound like someone clicking a light switch on and off, on and off. The boy's window is open. His sheets are twisted around his legs. If the boy was the kind of boy who sweats, surely his forehead would be slick with the stuff, but he almost never sweats, not unless he's outside in direct sunlight, another thing he's glad no one knows about him and never will. He sits up, listens. The boy agrees with the thoughts in his head that wish him to know he didn't hear a car crash after all. He heard something else. The fan falling on its side. A truck shifting into lower gear.

The boy turns the fan upright, steadies it atop the desk chair.

The fan blows air across his legs.

EIGHT

WHAT THE MOTHER tells the children is that they will be spending two weeks at Gumma's house. In Florida. Just the two of them. Without her.

"But how will we get to Florida?" the boy asks.

"Duh," the girl says. "In a plane."

"But," the boy says, "by ourselves?"

"So? It's no big deal," the girl says, even though she's sort of lying, because she too cannot imagine getting on a plane with her brother and ascending into the sky. Might as well launch the two of them to the moon.

"Your grandmother will meet you at the airport," the mother explains. "And the stewardesses know you're traveling without an adult. They'll keep an eye on you and make sure you get to where you're going." The mother tries to appear cheery, but the children detect a whiff of unease nonetheless. "Who knows?" she continues, "it might even be kind of fun?"

"I won't go!" the boy cries.

"Don't be a baby," the girl says. Then, "I'll protect you."

But on the day of the flight, the girl seems as nervous as the boy is. Their mother waits with them at the gate and even accompanies them down the jetway, where a smiling stewardess introduces herself as JoAnn and promptly gifts them each with captain's wings, a model plane, and an airplane activity book she knows they're going to love. "Now tell Mom you love her and that JoAnn is going to take great care of you, OK?" JoAnn says.

"We love you," the boy says.

"Bye, Mom," the girl says.

The mother holds them tight. Cries a little. Says she loves them. Makes them promise to call her when they get there.

"We promise," the girl says.

"JoAnn is going to take great care of us," the boy says, and everyone laughs, except the boy, who sometimes doesn't get what people think is funny.

But the boy is right: JoAnn does take great care of them. JoAnn brings them snacks and drinks. JoAnn replaces a dull crayon with a brighter one. She can also explain everything, which is sort of nice. When the plane dips, JoAnn says, "That's just light chop," and when the plane seems to be bouncing on a diving board, JoAnn says, "Just means we're winning the battle with good ol' gravity!" And when the captain announces he's going to leave the fasten seat belt light on for the remainder of the flight, JoAnn says, "Just a precaution, but let me know if you need me to walk you to the bathroom, OK?" The children pour ginger ale over ice cubes the shape of broken teeth. Ginger ale is a treat for the children, who prefer cola, but up here, at thirty-thousand feet, ginger ale is the sudden drink of choice, the one JoAnn recommends, the one nearly all the passengers seem to be drinking too. If only we flew around on planes all day, the girl thinks, Canada Dry would eclipse Coca-Cola.

When the plane arrives, JoAnn accompanies them to the gate. "Now, what does your grandma look like?" she asks.

The girl scans the group of people standing in the waiting area, one heartfelt reunion yielding to the next, and says, "We don't know."

JoAnn laughs, says, "Well, I'm sure your grandma will know what you two sweethearts look like."

"We never see her," the boy says.

"Well, that will make her so happy to see you then, I bet."

"She calls us on the phone," the boy says.

"Of course," JoAnn says. "That's what people do when they miss someone. Reach out and touch them, right?" JoAnn turns a cheer-leader smile on them, but the children glimpse the fear at its edges: the crowd is already starting to disperse, and Gumma is nowhere in sight. "Why don't we put our belongings over here," JoAnn says motioning them toward a kiosk, "and I'll make a quick phone call, OK?" While JoAnn speaks in whispers to another employee, the boy searches the thinning crowd, not so much for Gumma, but for anyone who might return the world to the one he knows. But the airport isn't like the world he knows, the boy is starting to learn, since it is fitted out with people pulling long-handled suitcases, the suitcase wheels spinning noisily across escalators that have forgotten to escalate and transport people from one side of the boy's vision to the other. The boy's first truth about airports: some-one, somewhere, is always running at full speed, at all times. Just turn your head to find the next one.

A few minutes later, JoAnn tells them she's sorry, she has to leave, but the other woman at the kiosk will take them to a special place where they can wait for their grandmother. "I'm so sad to say goodbye," JoAnn says, "but I know you two will have a wonderful time with your grandma." And the children are about to say good-bye too when Gumma materializes from wherever Gumma was, face red from exertion, breath heaving in her chest, and addresses not the children, who recognize her now from the last time they saw her—Gumma is Gumma is Gumma, the girl thinks—but JoAnn.

"They told me gate 38, so I go to gate 38," Gumma says, "and then they say, Oh, it's not gate 38 anymore; it's gate 14, but when I get to 14, they say, Go back to 38, and then 38 says they don't know which gate it is anymore. You want to talk about a runaround? This is a runaround. That's what I told the girl. I said, 'This is a real run-around, you know that?'"

JoAnn says she apologizes for the inconvenience; she knows how frustrating gate changes can be —

"They ought to *tell* you if they're going to change it! I said that to the girl. I said, 'You could have told us you were going to change it instead of making everyone run around like this!' I said, 'I'm the customer. Don't you care about the customer?' I said, 'Whatever happened to customer service?'"

JoAnn says they try to do everything they can to notify travelers about gate changes; she's sorry about the grandmother's ordeal.

"I said, 'Whatever happed to the customer always being right?' I said, 'Remember that?' Well, she didn't have anything to say about that. She just says, 'If you'd like to speak to my supervisor, I can call her.' And I said, 'I don't have time to speak to your supervisor!' I said, 'I've got two little grandchildren waiting for me! They're visiting me and I'm supposed to pick them up, and now I've spent all this time arguing with you, all because you couldn't tell people you were going to give us a runaround.' I said, 'Who knows where my grandkids are?' I said, 'Probably scared to death.' I said, 'You can tell your supervisor that.' Well, she didn't like me saying that, I could tell. Wouldn't even look at me. Just picked up the phone and pretended like she was talking to somebody, but I could tell there was nobody on the line. I said to her, I said, 'Tell your supervisor I said howdy,' and then I just got the hell out of there."

JoAnn says she's sorry, but she has to go now.

"Customer service is something you people need to learn something about," Gumma says. "That's for sure."

But JoAnn just smiles, gives the children a quick hug, and hurries off to the jetway. The children watch her go.

"I see your mother forgot to get haircuts for you two," Gumma says.

FLORIDA, second impressions: the heat! The way it arrests you from all sides, even from below, making socks obsolete, your feet strapped within a flip-flop, already slick with sweat the moment you fetch Gumma's mail from a mailbox shaped like a lighthouse. Palm trees, swaying limply in the infrequent breeze. The way sand gets between your toes even before you arrive at the beach. Thunderstorms so loud they rattle light fixtures, table lamps, silverware sheltering in a drawer. Driveways paved with crushed shells. The incredible variety of things that come in pink or turquoise; sofas, for example. Houses, for another. Seagulls following you for no real reason. The way your clothes smell like suntan lotion no matter how many times Gumma makes you put them through the wash. Sand in the washing machine. Sand in the dryer. Sand in the shower. Heat lightning.

A brown gecko riding the hood of the car, clinging to its shadow.

ON THE CHILDREN'S second day at Gumma's, Gumma takes them to a barber shop. "Imagine your mother sending you two down here with long hair hanging in your faces. Ridiculous."

"But my hair is *supposed* to be long," the girl protests. "That's the way I *like* it."

"Well," Gumma says, "maybe just a trim for you, girlie. But for this young man," she turns to the backseat where the boy is accompanying several stacks of magazines and newspapers to the salon, "for this young man, we're getting the works."

The works: a mustachioed barber instructs the boy to put his head down and works clippers through his spray-wet hair. Asks Gumma if he wants these sideburns trimmed up. Hands the boy a mirror the shape of a ping-pong paddle, says, "Here comes a lady-killer," and then liberates the boy from a black cape. The boy looks in the mirror. The barber powders the stranger there, works a talcum brush behind his now too-large ears.

The girl gets a one-inch trim she claims is too short and later gives in to the humiliation of crying, but only in bed when no one else is around, so it hardly even counts as crying at all.

———

IN THE EVENINGS, Gumma takes the children for a ride in her golf cart. The cart has two pedals, one ignition switch, and a fat steering wheel impaled on a black stick. A child's car. An implied automobile. The girl likes to sit up front with Gumma, the thrill of what's to come, while the boy prefers the back bench, where what's to come yields to what's already passed. Gumma drives with one hand on the wheel, the other cradles a plastic tumbler: a margarita, two teeny-tiny glasses of green mix, two teeny-tiny glasses of the clear stuff, topped with enough ice to make your hand go nearly numb—the girl is getting good at making Gumma's margarita, Gumma says. When they pass over speed bumps, the ice shifts within the tumbler.

Gumma drives them to a lake, a swimming pool, a tennis court, another lake, and a footbridge barely wider than the width of the cart, all without comment. They pass into an adjoining neighborhood, one with bigger houses spaced farther apart than the ones in Gumma's development. Here, large mossy trees trouble the sidewalks with thick roots. Carports yield to garages. Sprinklers, hidden within dense grass, tend yards whose edges are as stark and defined as the borders on a map. Gumma slows the cart before a house with a long driveway, pulls up to the curb. A newspaper, bundled with a red rubber band, rests on the driveway. Gumma turns to the boy and says, "Well, go get it."

"The newspaper?"

"The newspaper."

"Why?"

"A friend of mine asked me to pick it up for them," Gumma says.

"Why?"

"Because," Gumma says.

"You shouldn't steal," the girl says.

Gumma takes a sip from the tumbler. "Shouldn't do lots of things."

"Fine," girl says. "But if anyone catches us, I'm going to say it was your idea."

Gumma smiles. "Good plan," she says.

"There's no law against picking up a newspaper," the boy says, turning to Gumma for support, but Gumma only motions him toward the driveway, chews a large ice cube, swallows it, and says, "Try running."

The boy runs. As he does at the next house and the house after that. Three houses, three newspapers. The girl folds her arms across her chest and says she never wants to ride in the golf cart again. By the fourth house, the boy and Gumma have gotten the routine down to where Gumma only has to slow the cart without stopping. The boy pumps his arms for what seems the first time. Turns out, that's the secret of how to run faster: you've got to pump your arms. The boy runs, laughs.

———

BY THE END of their first week at Gumma's, bedtime has sort of disappeared altogether. Yes, the children can go to bed if they want and, yes, there's a bed for each of them and, yes, they know that's what they probably should do, but why go to bed when you can stay up late and watch grown-up TV in Gumma's living room? Shows where someone often ends up standing in a bedroom doorway witnessing something they're not supposed to witness; the camera zooms in, to capture their surprise. Shows without children in them. Shows where, at any moment, someone might call someone else a *son of a bitch* or shoot someone in the chest, an exit wound blooming across a wall. The children fall asleep on the sofa, the floor.

Mornings, their grandmother's coffee maker clears its throat, rouses them from dull dreams.

———

THEIR FATHER CALLS. How are they? They are fine, they say. The girl is on the bedroom phone; the boy is on the kitchen line. How's Florida? Florida is also fine. Hot, but fine. Well, their father says, there's no getting around that. True, they agree. And how is Gumma? She's fine too, the boy says. She's right here, do you want to talk to her? No, that's OK, the father says. I want to talk to you two. Oh, the children say. Tell me something you did today, their father says.

"We rode in a golf cart," the boy volunteers. "Real fast."

"Oh?" their father says. "Is that right?" But the children can tell he isn't really paying attention. The way his voice gets, like it's trying to climb a high step.

"Gumma lets him drive," the girl says.

"Does she? Well, how about that."

"I can reach the pedals," the boy says.

"Can not," the girl says. "Gumma has to help him."

"Can too!"

"Can not!"

"Can too!"

"Guys," their father says, "cool it. Let's have a nice conversation, OK? Does that sound OK to you two?"

"OK," the children say.

"Good. That's better. Now let's get back to our nice conversation."

"OK."

The children have never talked to their father across state lines before. Is there any end to separation's offer of the unprecedented? No, the girl decides later that evening, when she expertly twists a lime into Gumma's margarita. No, there is not.

———

THE BOY'S FEET do reach the golf cart's pedals; he has to sit at the edge of the seat and stretch his legs, uncomfortable, but worth it. In this manner, he tours Gumma's neighborhood. The feeling of driving! The boy navigates bike paths and cul-de-sacs, crosses the footbridge that yields to the neighborhood golf course, and then circles the course, presses the pedal, lets the wind take his hair. There's a hill near the eighteenth hole the boy likes to take full speed. The cart judders; the wheel shakes beneath the boy's hands. His stomach pleasantly lurches. The boy laughs. Imagines Alan and Chris watching him in awe, amazement. They can't believe what a daredevil the boy has become. "He's quite the daredevil, isn't he?" the boy imagines Alan saying, his imagination supplying Alan with a British accent while it's at it.

"Yes, I'd say so," Chris concurs, then pulls thoughtfully on a Sherlock Holmes pipe. "I'd say so."

———

ONE NIGHT, Gumma instructs the children to send their mother a postcard. She sets them up at the kitchen table, finds a pen for each of them, hands the girl an ancient-looking plastic bag, and says, "I'll get stamps tomorrow."

The girl opens the bag. Postcards, in various degrees of aging, some with names and addresses already written in, some with salutations (*Dear Fran and Johnnie; Howdy Iris; For Aunt Dorothea*), some already begun (*Well, it's hotter than blazes here, but we're eating our weight in ice cream and pop*), some complete (*PS: I don't know where you bought the fudge you sent me, but don't ever send that kind again. Worst fudge I ever tasted!*).

"But," the girl protests, "these aren't even Florida postcards."

"Sure they are," Gumma says. She's already sitting in front of the TV in her special chair, a La-Z-Boy recliner the children have been forbidden to use. When Gumma pulls a handle, her feet kick into the air like one of those wooden soccer players from that maddening game where the ball keeps rolling through. "They're from Florida, aren't they?"

"But the pictures," the girl says.

"The pictures are the best part," Gumma says. "That's why they call them picture postcards."

"They do?" the boy says, but Gumma has already turned up the volume the way she does.

The girl selects a blank postcard that shows an old-timey cartoon couple kissing on the sofa. *My Sweetie Gives Those 7 Day Kisses—They Make One Weak!* the postcard proclaims. The girl flips the card over and writes *Dear Mom* in her careful script. *How are you? We are having fun. It's so hot here!* The girl considers what else to include. She only has enough space for a few more sentences. *Sorry about this silly postcard*, she writes. *Isn't it dumb? I don't even get it. Oh well, I hope you like it anyway!*

The boy finds a nearly blank postcard (*Dear someone* has written) whose front reads *Greetings from Yuma Arizona, Year Round Agricultural Center.* The boy likes to keep his terrible handwriting to a minimum, so he tells his mom he's having fun, but misses her, and saves the remainder of the postcard for a fairly respectable drawing of Darth Vader sort of killing Obi-Wan Kenobi. *Ben?* he writes beneath Obi-Wan's vacant robe. *BEN! NO!*

"What would you two say to us having some juicy hamburgers tonight for dinner?" Gumma says from the recliner.

"Yay!" the boy says.

"Sounds good," the girl agrees.

"Great," Gumma says. "There's ground beef in the fridge and buns in the cabinet above the microwave." She closes her eyes and tells them she's going to take a little nap before dinner. "And make sure not to press down too hard on the spatula. That's how you lose all the juices."

———

THE CHILDREN get sunburned. The girl's nose begins to peel. The boy's pale tummy reddens, except for one spot just above his belly button, a fold of skin that ducks the sun whenever the boy sits in the wet apron of sand at the surf's edge and builds castles. The spot looks like a smiley face's smile.

"You have a smiley face!" his sister teases, points. "Smiley face!"

"Do not," the boy protests. But he tells himself that tomorrow he must remember to lie flat in the sun to burn the smile away.

———

ONE MORNING, the boy is driving the cart through the neighborhood when he sees their cat sunning itself on a driveway. That's impossible, the boy thinks. But the cat raises its head when the boy calls its name and blinks its familiar eyes in what seems clear recognition. I knew you would follow us to Florida! the boy thinks. The cat yawns, as if to say, Yes, that's absolutely correct. Some joker has affixed a red flea collar to the cat's neck; their cat only wears white flea collars. The boy calls the cat again, but the cat ignores him.

THE GIRL cannot send Sarah a postcard. She wants to send Sarah a postcard, but how? She can't send it to her father's apartment without having to ask her mother for the address, and she can't ask her mother for the address without her mother asking why she wants the address, and she can't tell her mother she wants the address so she can send Sarah a postcard without hurting her mother's feelings, and so, no matter how much the girl would like to send Sarah a postcard, and no matter how much the girl knows Sarah would like receiving one, the girl cannot send Sarah a postcard.

THE CHILDREN get good at making Gumma's margaritas. The secret, Gumma tells them, is letting the ice melt just enough to cut the flavor of the lime without getting too watery. Drink after the melt, but before the water. "Should be a bumper sticker," Gumma muses. The three of them ride through the neighborhood late in the evening. Passing cars afford them a wide berth, their drivers giving them a quick, sidelong look, this grandmother out with her grandchildren well after bedtime, showing off her stupid golf cart, no doubt, the kids enthralled, impressed, too dumb to know they should be back home in bed. How unhappy some lives are! So true, but what can anyone do about it? Nothing, aside from slow down to a safe crawl and pass safely on the left.

They enter the nicer neighborhood, as the children think of it now. They pass the house where Gumma first instructed the boy to retrieve the newspaper—two cars stand in the driveway, no newspaper in sight—and pass another with its interior lights on, a sprinkler darkly waving from a flowerbed. For a moment the girl thinks the sprinkler got them, but it's just the air doing that to her skin, the way the air always does down here, even in the morning, when it's not even hot yet, and the girl's tank top adheres to the small of her back. Cruel air. Mean state. The girl will not miss Florida, she thinks, then realizes she's really thinking she won't miss Gumma but feels guilty for thinking that. One day, people are going to know the girl's thoughts, and then the jig will be up.

Gumma stops in front of a house whose lights are off, lawn overgrown, mailbox door open like a slack jaw. "Those plants," Gumma says. She nods to the porch, where a dozen potted plants congregate around a wicker bench. "Bring me a tall one."

The girl turns to her brother says, "Don't do it." Glimpses the uncertainty in his eyes—her brother has a poker face that wouldn't cut it in tiddlywinks.

"If the tall ones are too heavy, a smaller one is fine."

The girl says, "You know it's stealing."

"People go on vacation and leave their plants to die," Gumma says. "We're not stealing, we're rescuing."

The boy smiles, and the girl understands that she's lost him to Gumma again. So be it. Fine. What does she care? She will fold her arms across her chest while her brother crosses the lawn, ascends the porch, and fails to lift a tall plant from its planter. Will she say a word when her brother says he's almost got it; can she help him lift it? No, she will not. Because—and here's the thing her brother has yet to figure out—there's power in saying no. Real and true and actual power. Because "no" is just about the most powerful word in the dictionary, as far as the girl is concerned. But her brother is still stuck on "yes," a child's word. The call to arms of the weak, the hesitant, and the eager-to-please. Well, the girl is beyond all that. She's moving on to other things, she is.

And that's why it's OK for her to help her brother carry a heavy plant across the yard. Because she's moving on to other things, while her brother tarries in wherever it is he's tarrying in—the girl doesn't even care really.

"We got the biggest one," the boy says, the moment they heave the plant into the golf cart.

Gumma downs the last of her margarita. "Careful," she says. "They tip real easy."

———

ON THE DAY the children are to leave, Gumma drives them to the airport and gives them a ten-dollar bill. "In case you get hungry," she says. A ten-dollar bill. Birthday card–level money. Enough to open their father's coin bank even. But the girl says she'll keep the money in her purse in case of an emergency, which the boy says is the dumbest plan ever.

"Let's split it," he says.

"No," the girl says.

"Aw, come on!"

The girl doesn't say anything.

"It's no fair. Gumma said it was for both of us. Gumma said it was for snacks."

"Gumma said," the girl says. "Gumma said."

"I'm telling," the boy says, but who would he tell? Another truth about your parents separating and your mom sending you to Florida to spend time with your grandmother who must drop you off at the airport and give you money for your flight home: there are fewer and fewer people to tell.

But a few minutes before departure, the girl relents when the boy wants to waste his half on M&Ms and a stuffed bear three years too young for him. The bear sports sunglasses and a baseball mitt. Let him have it, the girl thinks. Why not? And it isn't until they board the plane and another exuberant stewardess showers them with the same gifts they received on the first flight that the girl realizes she didn't even kiss Gumma goodbye, which makes her cry a little. The plane terrifyingly ascends into a pink sky. The girl misses Gumma, misses Florida. Even misses the golf cart. Why is everything so sort of terrible?

NINE

THE CHILDREN have only been back home for two days when their mother tells them there's somebody she'd like them to meet.

"Ha!" the girl says, louder than she intended. Her mother and brother look at her.

"Is something funny?" her mother asks. Her voice does that thing where it tells you she's deciding whether to be angry; you have control. Choose wisely.

"No," the girl says. But the girl remembers the last time she heard that line. If this is about her mom dating some guy, well, that's pretty much the last thing in the world the girl would like to hear about right now, it really is. Just when she was doing such a great job keeping her admiration for Sarah a secret, playing it cool, surprising her father with her acceptance of his girlfriend — a daughter who accepts her recently separated father's dating someone new, go check the record books for that one — and now this. Dating, part two. Because that's exactly what her mother is telling them now: she's been spending time with someone who has a son their age, and now she wants to know if they would be comfortable meeting him. The son, she means. Marcus. And his father, Cliff.

"Cliff?" the girl says.

"Yes," the mother says.

"Like Clifford," the boy volunteers. "The big red dog?"

"Ha," the girl says.

"Something funny?" the mother says.

The girl says no. But she can't stop laughing. The kind of laughter that haunts her at school: in the middle of a filmstrip, the class-room lights turned low, the filmstrip dull, tedious, yet accidentally hilarious too, the way it has no idea how bored they all are, watching it, even as the teacher keeps instructing them to quiet down, even as the filmstrip beams brightly on, which only serves to make the girl feel that she's about to laugh too, along with everyone else who has already given in. That's the thing about this kind of laughter: it always wins in the end. Now, standing before her mother and brother, the girl loses it again, the way she knew she would all along.

"You, room, now," the mother says. Which is also funny, but the girl manages to make it upstairs before giving in.

———

THE FATHER has a hard time paying attention to the children, but the boy is only starting to catch on to that, now that he and his sister have returned from Florida. The father asks the boy questions about their trip, about Gumma, about all the fun things they did together, but doesn't pay attention to the boy's answers. It's sad, the way his father can't quite pay attention, the boy thinks, without the least feeling of anger. His poor dad, wanting to be nice, wanting to be a good dad who asks his children questions, who listens, who takes time to let his children know how much they matter to him—all that. See him now with his hands on the wheel, asking his son what fun things they did together in Florida. See him nod when his son breathlessly recalls the time he got the golf cart up to nearly twenty miles an hour by driving it down this hill on the other side of the golf course, this real steep hill, that has like, a golf cart path on one side and then, like, a road on the other? Well, what the boy did was drive the golf cart to the top of the hill and then wait until there weren't any cars around—he didn't want to anyone to see him racing the golf cart down the steep hill—and then he pressed down on the pedal and steered the cart down the middle of the path because the middle of the path was, like, smoother than the other part of the path, and by the time he got to the bottom of the hill, the speedometer said twenty miles an hour because the golf cart had a speedometer in it just like a real car.

"A speedometer in a golf cart?" the father says, then makes a right-hand turn. "Not sure why you'd need that."

———

SOMETHING IS up with Sarah. The girl isn't sure what it is, but ever since the girl returned from Florida, Sarah has been acting differently. Quieter. Harder to read. Take today, for example. Sarah drives the girl to the mall, even though they don't really need anything at the mall. Sarah tells the girl she wants to check out some sales, and the girl says OK, sure, let me get my shoes on. The drive to the mall: a series of silences broken only by the girl changing radio stations—Sarah, unlike the girl's father, lets her choose what they listen to—and the girl's halfhearted attempts to draw Sarah into some pleasant chitchat. But Sarah only nods politely when the girl says she wants to find a pair of sunglasses or mentions the dog watching them from the pickup truck in the next lane. The girl changes the station. Sarah taps a finger against the steering wheel. So much of the girl's life is spent in the company of an adult driving her somewhere.

At the mall, Sarah asks the girl if she would like to get a drink at Orange Julius. The girl loves Orange Julius, especially their piña coladas, so sweet and sugary and delicious that the girl must remind herself not to finish them in two minutes flat, the way she always does.

"OK," the girl says, "but don't you want to shop a little first?"

"Shop?"

"The sales."

"Oh," Sarah says. "We'll always have the sales."

The two them sit in the food court together, an eatery dominated primarily by children affixed to drinks with thick red straws, their posture conveying a strong desire to simultaneously sit and not sit at the table, while their parents urge napkins, condiments, criticism on them. A glass elevator rises from a fountain, applauding itself over and over again, its bottom jeweled with pennies. The girl reminds herself not to finish the piña colada too soon, even though she's already finished, which is what always happens with the piña coladas. The only decent thing to do now is navigate the straw through several strata of tasty ice and foam. It's incredible how good this tastes, but the girl adopts an expression that attempts to convey boredom, indifference.

After a while, Sarah says, "So."

"So," the girl says.

But Sarah doesn't say anything. She sips her Orange Julius and watches the glass elevator shepherd a family from the food court to the galleria level, a mother and three children, the children pressing their faces to the glass the way the girl used to when to she was little — the girl is watching them too because Sarah is and because what else is she going to do? It's funny how fast the elevator scoots the three children up to the galleria, while their expressions remain unchanged, unaware how many people are watching them. For a moment, the girl longs to be a little kid again on the glass elevator, but she doesn't really, and the moment passes.

"Ready?" Sarah asks, even though she hasn't finished her drink.

"Yeah," the girl says.

But when the girl heads back toward the mall, Sarah says, "Oh, I thought we were leaving."

"Oh."

"Unless you wanted to stay?"

"No, that's OK."

"Sure?"

The girl nods.

"OK."

On the drive home, Sarah lingers too long at a stop sign, too dutifully checks left, then right, then left again. "Go ahead," she says, to a driver waiting across the intersection. "Yes, you." Sarah motions her hand for the driver to pass through. The driver, a woman with a headscarf, waves as she passes. But even after the headscarf woman is gone, Sarah does not pass through the intersection. The girl turns the radio on, finds a station. Another car materializes at the intersection. Sarah waves it through, waits, then finally accelerates.

And it isn't until the girl is in bed that night that she realizes Sarah must have wanted to talk to her about something.

————

QUESTION: is there a difference between going to the dentist when your parents are together and going to the dentist when they're not? Answer: the boy isn't sure. He still fears the dentist, still brushes his teeth like a madman the morning of the appointment, still experiences an approximate three hundred percent increase in flossing in the days leading up to the appointment, and still finds no comfort whatsoever in Dr. Solano's waiting room, which has been painted to resemble an ecstatic ocean teeming with smiling swordfish, grinning crabs, and brace-faced whales. Chairs shaped like shells. Office windows tricked out like portholes. In a tall aquarium suffused with purple light, a dozen real fish, not in on the act, stare implacably from behind thick glass.

When it is the boy's turn, Dr. Solano's assistant seats him in the exam chair, affixes an embarrassing bib around his neck, and then begins addressing a long-nosed piece of medical equipment as "Pinocchio," as in "We're just going to let Pinocchio take a look inside your mouth" and "Pinocchio helps us get a super look at your gums" and "Pinocchio tells us you're doing a great job brushing—no cavities today!" Later, the assistant scrapes his teeth with a pitchfork and tells him about her summer travel plans. Next week, they're taking the whole family to Hershey Park and then going down the shore the week after that. "My kids don't want summer to end!" the assistant assures him, in case the boy might be in doubt.

From the adjoining room, the boy can hear his sister arguing with Dr. Solano. His sister always argues with Dr. Solano. She doesn't want to get a cavity filled; why does she have to get her cavity filled today? Her tooth feels fine. Dr. Solano sends the boy's assistant to go fetch their mother from the waiting room. A few moments later, their mother enters the adjoining room—the boy can hear the three of them arguing, an argument the mother is sure to win; the girl will get her cavity filled today. A few moments later, the boy hears the drill, Dr. Solano's unconsoling consolation. The boy feels tears form in the corners of his eyes.

"That's your sister over there," Dr. Solano says later, when he stops by to glance inside the boy's mouth. "Crying like a bee stung her."

The boy has always been the luckier of the two. No cavities. No broken bones. No visits to the emergency room, as his sister has done, twice already, once when she fell from a swing set, the other time when she got a peppermint candy lodged in her throat. The boy remembers that incident. He rode in the back seat with his sister while their mother drove them to the hospital at breakneck speeds, occasionally glancing back, saying "it'll be OK" and "almost there" and "everything's going to be fine." But his sister's expression conveyed only moderate surprise, as if she too were as nonplussed as everyone else about why they were speeding through traffic lights and intersections, her face slowly ripening like a bagged fruit.

———

BUT WHAT ARE their arguments really about? That's what the father would like to know. Because when you get right down to it, it seems like their arguments are really about not much of anything. Just the normal disagreements between two people who have passed through the earliest stages of getting to know one another—those superficial layers, so thin, so flimsy, so full of the easy and the empty—and are now testing out the deeper layers of actually knowing another person, where things naturally get a little rockier, right? That's to be expected. That's not surprising. So they argue sometimes, sure. But—and this is the thing the father thinks is the heart of the matter—what are their arguments really *about*?

"They're about two things," Sarah says. "The way you see the world vs. the way I see the world."

"I don't know what that means," the father says.

"It means exactly what it means," Sarah says.

"'It means exactly what it means?'" the father says. "There's nothing I can do with that. What I am supposed to do with that?"

Sarah says, "You can do whatever you want with that."

The father feels the way he often feels when he argues with Sarah—namely, that he is losing a game whose rules have never been fully explained to him, a game like the ones he used to toss from the children's playroom, whose boxes had lost their tops, tokens missing, the boards as fascinating and useless as maps of the moon.

"'You can do whatever you want with that,'" the father says. "Wow. Thanks. Great. That's really helping things."

"Oh, poor me," Sarah says. "I'm just trying to be helpful, and everyone else won't play fair."

"That's not what I said."

"Oh, no, everyone is misconstruing what I said. Wah. Poor me."

"If you're not going to be reasonable."

"He said," Sarah says, "then suddenly realized he was full of crap."

"I don't have to take this."

"He said, playing the victim."

"I'm not playing anything! I'm just trying to talk to you. Christ!"

"Are you?" Sarah says. "You might want to think about that."

"All I am trying to do is have a reasonable conversation with you that doesn't devolve into insults and arguments."

"He said, meaning the exact opposite."

"Fine!" the father says. "You've got me dead to rights. You really have. I have not been trying to have a reasonable conversation that doesn't devolve into an argument. Instead, I'm only trying to paint myself as a victim and draw you into a fight. There? Happy?"

Sarah says, "No, but glad to see you figuring things out."

————

THE NEXT TIME the babysitter babysits the children, he donates thirty-five cents to the coin bank. "Finding money is super easy," he says. "All you have to do is, like, pick stuff up and move stuff around, and you'll find some money." That's what the babysitter did to find the change: he ripped the floor mats from his car, scooped the contents of the glove box into a garbage bag, yanked the carpet from the trunk, lifted the spare tire from the spare tire compartment, and then dug his fingers underneath the compartment. When he was done searching his car, he went through his house, pulled every kitchen drawer free, dragged sofas from the wall, moved coffee tables and end tables from their usual places, rolled area rugs away from windows, and inspected the washer and dryer with a flashlight. "That's where I found the money," he says. "The dryer."

"What about the other places?" the girl asks.

The babysitter shrugs. "Nothing," he says. "But there could have been."

———

ONE SATURDAY, the children accompany their mother to Lums Pond, where they are to meet Cliff and Marcus. The children do not want to meet Cliff and Marcus. The children do not want to go to Lums Pond. Why, the girl wonders, is life so often a matter of answering yes to things you'd rather say no to? The boy sits beside her, wrapped in his own worry. For one thing, he's scared of Lums Pond, which is so forcibly full of nature, nature including snakes, frogs, turtles, spiders, spiderwebs, poison ivy, murky water, weeds, briars, ants, and those little sharp pebbles that invariably creep into the boy's socks and harass his feet. For another, the boy doesn't know what to call Cliff—Cliff, Mr. Cliff, Mr. Cliff's last name, whatever it is—and decides, as they pull into the parking lot, that he will not call him anything at all. Nine hundred times out of ten, the boy is starting to realize, the best way to deal with a problem is to avoid it altogether.

They meet at the boat rental office.

The boy's first impression of Marcus: taller than expected. Super skinny. Mouth bulged with gum.

The girl's first impression of Cliff: those glasses, those shorts— do they still make shorts like those?—that shirt. Let's not even mention the teeth. Although the girl sometimes feels guilty for thinking this way, lately it's like she divides the world into attractive people and not quite attractive people. Terrible habit, but hers and no one else's to know.

Marcus: the first kid the boy has ever met who wears a necklace.

Marcus says "hey" to the girl's "hi," nods to her "nice to meet you."

They decide to rent two canoes since, as a ponytailed teen explains, it's easier to navigate in groups of two or three. And the boy tries to mask his unease when, instead of dividing up between Cliff and Marcus in one canoe and the children and their mother in the other, Marcus suggests they put the kids in one canoe and the adults in the other, an idea their mother strangely and disappointingly approves of. The teen hands the boy a damp life jacket the approximate weight of a junked tire. Tells him to put it on. Adjusts the shoulders. The jacket has five confusing straps and seven bewildering clasps, a puzzle the teen solves in an instant. "Don't pull on anything," the teen says cryptically, and the boy nods. For the boy, all day there is the sensation of being in the life jacket, a slick-wet suffocation that accompanies him after he returns the jacket, after he asks the teen where he should put it, and the teen, without looking at him, says, "There's a sign, read the sign," and points to a handwritten sign taped to the cash register that reads LIFE JACKETS HERE! DO NOT FOLD!

The adults help the children into a canoe. The canoe rocks and leans. Waves chuckle against its dented hull. The boy steps inside; a brown puddle accepts his unsteady feet. The boy's shoes are wet. His socks are wet. The boy turns to his mother to see whether she might relent and let him go with her, but she only hands him an oar and says, "Here you go, big guy," and the boy understands "big guy," a name she's never called him before, to be a tacit signal that he is to pretend to enjoy himself in his canoe while she will pretend to enjoy herself in hers. "OK," the boy says, and takes the oar, lighter than he imagined.

"You can steer the ship," his mother says, brightly.

"I'm steering," Marcus says, seating himself at the rear of the canoe while the boy's sister grabs the middle seat — the driest seat — and passes her oar back to Marcus. Cliff tells Marcus to wait until they're ready to follow them, but Marcus is already pushing off from the boat landing. The boy didn't realize you could use an oar to push off, but of course you can, Marcus's gesture would have him know, of course you can.

"Marcus," Cliff warns. "Wait for us to catch up."

But Marcus is making a series of badge-worthy J-strokes, laughing, and for the first time the boy truly understands the phrase *glide through water*. When the boy puts his oar in the water, Marcus calls out, "Don't! You'll just slow us down." The boy nods assent. The oar, wetly raised from the sunlit water, looks like it's raining electricity.

"Try to stay down," Marcus says.

The boy, sitting as low as he possibly can, sits even lower.

"Don't listen to him," the girl tells him. "He's just showing off."

"Wind resistance," Marcus says. "Ever heard of it?"

"Give me a break," the girl says.

"You need to stay down too."

But the girl only laughs and, against Marcus's orders, places her oar in the water and starts counter-paddling.

"Hey! Don't do that!" Marcus says.

The girl switches the oar to the other side, drops it in, and says, "Do what?"

In this manner they reach the center of the pond, Marcus yelling at the girl to stop that, executing stroke after stroke, the girl dropping the oar into the water in a desultory way that really doesn't slow them down, the boy realizes, but hands the girl yet another victory nonetheless. She's good at winning even when she's losing, his sister is, another maddening quality to add to all the others. The three of them rock in the pond's puny wake. The water exudes the smell of damp leaves. Marcus steers them alongside a row of wooden posts inexplicably rising from the water's surface and says, "Sometimes you can find turtles here." And, as if to prove Marcus right, a fat turtle materializes atop a post and blinks its creepy eyes at the boy. "Careful he doesn't bite you," Marcus laughs, and that's when the boy realizes he's cowering— when did he start doing that? Marcus steers the canoe toward the turtle and knocks it off the post with his oar. The turtle splashes into water, heavy as a stone. "Stupid turtle," Marcus says.

"What did he ever do to you?" the girl says.

"Acted stupid," Marcus says, steering them to another turtle and knocks it off the post. "That's what."

"Maybe he thinks you act stupid."

The boy looks to Marcus to see if he's angry, but Marcus smiles, says, "What he thinks is what he thinks."

In the distance, the boy can see his mother and Cliff paddling toward them. His mother has her back turned, talking to Cliff, who occasionally cups his hand to his eyes, looking for the three of them, even though he has to see them, right? He's close enough that the boy can see the lettering on his T-shirt, but not the words. "I think they're looking for us," the boy volunteers.

Marcus says, "Your dad left you?"

"He didn't leave," the girl says.

"Yeah," the boy says. "He moved to an apartment."

"That means he left you," Marcus says.

"We see him all the time," the girl says.

"Sure," Marcus says, "but he still left you."

"Shut up!" the girl says.

"No big deal," Marcus says. "My dad left too."

"He didn't leave!" the girl says.

"Moved away, whatever," Marcus says. "That's how it always starts. The apartment. The apartment is fun," Marcus continues, "at first." He steers them toward a stand of posts, each one topped with a sleeping turtle. Easy prey. "Then the next thing is the girlfriend. Your dad got one of those?"

"Shut up!" the girl screams, and reaches for Marcus's oar.

"That means yes?"

"Shut your stupid face!" the girl says, and in an impressive move, grabs Marcus's oar and hurls it into the water all in one motion. A surprise: the oar floats.

"It always starts with the girlfriend," Marcus says. "That'll turn south soon enough."

"You don't know what you're talking about," the girl says.

"Yeah? Just stay tuned then," Marcus says. "Your dad's little ol' girlfriend will be saying adios soon enough. Always do."

And the boy is disappointed when the girl doesn't say anything back. Instead, she stares away in the opposite direction. I'm not even here, her posture says.

Marcus borrows the boy's oar and knocks three turtles off in a row—plunk, plunk, plunk—as easily as a protagonist in a video game. Then he steers the canoe toward the tossed oar and instructs the boy to grab it. The boy reaches but can't quite get the oar without leaning too far from the boat.

"Grab it!" Marcus shouts.

But the boy cannot permit himself to reach out far enough, and, after a few passes, Marcus fishes the oar from the water.

TEN

THE GIRL HAS more trouble sleeping at night. Through her bedroom wall, she can hear her mother's snoring. Down the hall, her brother's fan, turning invisibly on its base, seems to be asking the same question over and over again: *how? how? how?* If the girl puts her arms on top of her sheets, her arms feel too cold; if she pulls the sheets to her chin, the rest of her body feels too hot. A compromise: the girl turns on her side and frees one leg from the sheets, her foot free, liberated. But what to do about her ear, which grows warm against the pillow?

The girl tries to pray, but it's no use. She goes through the Our Father, Hail Mary, and Glory Be, all without feeling or comfort. Terrible the way the Hail Mary ends with *now and at the hour of our death*, the girl thinks. Awful. And that business about *the fruit of thy womb*, which always makes the girl think of Fruit of the Loom underwear, even when the girl senses that line coming and tells herself she will not think of Fruit of the Loom but knows she's going to fail again since she's already thinking about it just by thinking she shouldn't be thinking about it. And the Our Father: why, oh why would God ever *lead us into temptation* enough that we might need to ask him not to do so?

But the thing the girl should absolutely not think about now if she wants to fall asleep is the knowledge that, all around her, from her home to her neighbors' homes and to the homes beyond that, everyone is lying down in a horizontal position on a soft slab the world calls a "bed," with a soft cushion beneath their heads called a "pillow," trying to give human consciousness the slip, a pursuit no one seems to find in the least bit strange.

———

THIS IS THE summer of finding lighters in parking lots, but nobody knows that except the boy. He finds a blue one in his father's apartment complex lot and a yellow one at the supermarket when his mother tells him to return their cart. The boy loves steering the shopping cart across the parking lot. Enjoys sending it crashing into the others, the way the other carts resist, then yield.

Usually, the lighters are out of lighter fluid. Push down, hold, and the lighter releases a temporary spark. But the yellow one is still in business. Aha, the flame seems to say. The boy presses down until his thumb gets burned. Drops the lighter, then inspects the burn. A little black half-crescent, like a magic marker's leavings, but deeper, darker. Painful. The boy's first thought: he's got to show Marcus this.

———

THEIR FATHER never comes with them to the pool anymore, just Sarah. They don't even talk about it really; now it is understood, the girl realizes, that the three of them will go to the pool while the father hangs back at the apartment, doing work or whatever it is he does. Sarah packs the children's pool gear into a canvas bag and throws the bag across her shoulder. "Ready?" she says.

The girl gets good at diving.

The boy finds two quarters in the deep-end drain and promises to put them in the coin bank, but the promise somehow gives him permission to invest them elsewhere, and so he deposits them in the poolside vending machine which, unlike the bank, immediately rewards him with a treat: Michigan Cherries.

"Those are terrible for you," Sarah says.

"Yeah," the girl agrees.

Still, Sarah ends up having one anyway, so of course his sister has one too, and since no one can eat just one Michigan Cherry, they end up polishing off the bag together, their fingers unnaturally red.

The boy gets better at holding his breath underwater. The secret: clamp your nose with your fingers. It's OK to do that if no one is looking. Which most people aren't. Underwater, at least.

The three of them get good at going to the pool together.

———

WHAT THE MOTHER tells her friend is that she wants this phase to be over.

"What phase?"

The early phase, the mother explains. The before phase.

"Well," the friend laughs, "that's easy enough to do."

The mother says that's not what she means. "I want to stop being hypersensitive about everything I say, everything I do. You know?"

The friend says she does not know.

"How could you not know?" the mother asks.

"Out of practice?"

"Oh," the mother says. "Well, that's not a bad thing."

"It sort of is," her friend says. "All my friends are separating. It's crazy. Not *crazy* crazy. Sorry."

The mother tells her not to worry, it *is* crazy.

"I mean," her friend says, "and don't take this the wrong way, OK, because it's going to come off maybe sounding the wrong way, but sometimes it's like I can barely stand to talk to my separated friends anymore."

The mother says, "We're not exactly a club, you know."

"See? I told you it would come off wrong."

"There's no little club jacket they give you. No little membership card. At least, I haven't gotten mine yet."

"That's not what I meant."

"I know. I'm just giving you a hard time."

"Well, don't do that," the friend says. "You know I have a hard time telling when you're kidding or not."

"I know. Sorry."

"And I don't do well with teasing."

So take a pass on being alive, the mother thinks, but says, "I'll stop teasing."

"Thank you."

Don't say, You're welcome. That's borderline kidding/teasing. Careful.

"All I meant is that sometimes it's hard for me to talk to my separated friends and not feel jealous of them. Is that terrible? But that's the way I feel sometimes, jealous. Because you get a break from parenting whenever your kids are at your ex's, and you go on dates and meet new people and, you know, just sort of get out and into the world. In a way I haven't in years. Prechildren, premarriage, I mean."

The mother says she doesn't exactly feel like she's getting out in the world. It's more like she's going on guarded dates with Cliff. "We went to Lums Pond."

"Oh."

"That's what getting out and into the world is like for us separated folks," the mother says, forgetting her promise. "Paddling a canoe around a smelly pond."

Her friend says, "Well, at least there's a pond."

The mother says, "You can have the pond."

"You're back to teasing."

"I'm back to being honest."

"Well, I was just trying to be honest too."

The mother says, "I know." Apologizes. Why does she always end up apologizing? Something she would ask Cliff if she weren't so busy steering the conversation away from his spending the night. "You know what I would like?" the mother says.

"What?"

"I would like to be in a room where nothing is required of me. Nothing. I'm just there in this room and no one has any expectations about me whatsoever."

"You mean, like a retirement home?"

But that's not at all what the mother means. What she means is being free of the daily labor of being a person, of meeting expectations, of being thought kindly of, of pleasing everyone else, of being a dutiful mother, friend, worker, student, neighbor, citizen, of beautifully striving for whatever, all while utterly failing to achieve whatever.

"Sort of," the mother says.

———

PEOPLE ARE stealing gas. Check the local news. Gas station owners say they don't know what to do. Not their job to be policemen, not their job to be the judge and jury, not their job to be security guards, they say. Don't get paid enough for all that work. But what would you do if people were stealing from you? In broad daylight? Grab a baseball bat, that's what. Grab a baseball bat and chase them down. Smash a window if you can. Make them pay, one way or another.

Outside the stations, lines as long as city blocks. Cars with doors swung wide. People pushing them that last empty half mile or more.

THE CHILDREN never ask the father about the separation. The father prepares himself nonetheless. He knows what he will say the moment the children ask him about it, as they certainly might, eventually, and he knows how he will speak to them, like they are nearly adults, even though that's not true and even though that might not be the way you're supposed to talk to your kids about the end of their parents' marriage—but what is the right way? That's what the father would like to know. There is no right way, is the answer. He will map out his own path, forge ahead, fly blind, wing it. When the children ask why the parents decided to separate, the father will let them know that's a good question, a question he has spent many sleepless nights thinking about, a question he still does not have the full answer for and may never, if he is to be honest with them, have the full answer for. But here is his best answer, he will say. And then he will tell the children, and they will listen and feel uncertain and fearful, but the father, being sharp and savvy, will have anticipated their fears and will know how to assuage them; he'll be good at that. He can be good at that sort of thing, after all. And the children will recognize he's doing a good job putting their fears at ease and will understand that, despite the separation, he is still their father and their protector and is still very much in charge, mostly, or at least occasionally. And the children will feel better having spoken to him and he will feel better having answered their questions. They will grow closer. They will gain a better understanding of one another because, if the father can be honest with them—and he imagines telling the children this too—being separated has given him the opportunity to really get to know them in a way that wasn't possible when they were all living in the house together. It's true. Because when he was living in the house with them, he had to go through the motions of his day, from a hurried breakfast, then off to work, then back home in the evening for a few heartfelt, but let's face it, ultimately superficial transactions with them. A quick game of catch on the front yard. A walk around the darkening neighborhood. A bedtime story. All wonderful stuff, sure, but the thing is, the father would explain—and this is the truth, the kind of truth he wouldn't have thought of sharing with them before the separation but that seems possible to express now—back when he lived in the house with them he was always aware of his role in the household as Father and strove to maintain that role ahead of actually getting to *know* the children as *people*. Just people like any other people the father might happen to know. Because yes, they are special people because they are his children, but they're also regular people too, with their own personalities, interests, tastes, preferences, habits, passions, aspirations, fears, doubts, worries, and so on. And that's what separation helped him see that marriage kept hidden: it would be important for him to get to know his children as people, not just as his children. That's something he's thankful for, really. Had he and their mother never separated, he would never have known. See?

The father imagines saying this to the children, but the children never ask him about the separation, so the father keeps imagining.

———

EVERY ONCE in a while, when they're spending the weekend at their father's, the boy will feel upset and scared and need to call his mother. Whenever this happens, the father sets the boy up in the master bedroom, where he can have some privacy. Says, "Take all the time you need." Closes the bedroom door. Still, the three of them can hear the boy crying behind the door. "I can't sleep here," he says between tears or "I was afraid you wouldn't be home" or "But I don't want to be here." The girl can't stand it when her brother gets this way. It makes her so angry. She thinks terrible and horrible things about him, but then she feels guilty for thinking that way and decides to let him slide, the little crybaby. World's going to swallow him whole.

THEY START going places with Marcus. First, a tedious movie together that bores all of them except the boy, who finds the exploits of a purple-haired dragon harrowing and hilarious. Next outing, a kids-eat-free pizza buffet, insulting to Marcus, who orders two calzones off the regular menu and a Caesar salad without the olives. Marcus tells the boy and girl that open buffets get sneezed on by everyone in town, he saw it on *60 Minutes*. "A giant peach-tree dish with tongs is what those things are," Marcus says, and the boy tries but fails to summon an image of a peach-tree dish. The third time, they attempt an outdoor screening of *The Wizard of Oz*, but it rains before Dorothy is not in Kansas anymore, and Marcus says he hates musicals anyway, which aren't realistic and would only make sense if everyone walked around drunk all day.

But what could possess them to go to Philadelphia during the hottest part of July? There the five of them stand—the boy, the girl, the mother, Cliff, and Marcus—sweating in line for the Liberty Bell, Independence Hall, and the Franklin Institute, where they later tour the terrifying interior of a beating heart and press their fingers to a glass globe branched with lightning. The children eat freeze-dried ice cream that comes sealed in triangular packets; Marcus shows them how to repurpose the packets as whoopee cushions. Cliff buys a half dozen soft pretzels from a street vendor, the pretzels wet to the touch, slick, glistening.

"You know what's on these?" Marcus says between bulging mouthfuls. "Embalming fluid."

"No there isn't," the girl says.

"What's embalming?" the boy asks.

"For dead people," Marcus says brightly, and takes another bite. "Mmm, yummy."

"That's stupid," the girl says, but she's stopped eating her pretzel.

"They put it on dead people?" the boy asks.

"To keep them preserved," Marcus explains.

"Oh."

"That's the stupidest thing I've ever heard," the girl says. But she's already tearing the pretzel into bits and tossing them onto the sidewalk. Pigeons gather, rip and tear at the leavings, their heads looking this way, that way, this. If there's anything scarier than pigeons, the boy doesn't know what it is. How does everyone act so casual around them? Like Marcus, for example, who now runs through the pigeons, chasing them creepily away, until Cliff yells at him to stop. The boy wouldn't run through pigeons for twenty dollars. Knows they wouldn't be afraid of him, their ugly beaks hungry for his eyes.

"Those pretzels will kill 'em," Marcus says, not without mirth.

"No they won't," the girl says. "Think about it. If that was true, you'd see dead pigeons *everywhere*."

"Well," Marcus says, "start looking."

The boy looks. He sees pigeons bobbing along window ledges and archways. He sees pigeons sheltering beneath railway bridges and bus stops, congregating around vendors, trash cans, and benches, none of them the least bit dead. Unless they die after he sees them. The boy considers this. The thing about Marcus is that he knows things, things not everybody else knows, and that's what drives the boy's sister crazy; Marcus knows things she doesn't. Like the way he spits on the sidewalk when their mother and Cliff aren't looking and says, "Ever get a bad taste in your mouth you can't get rid of? Well, just spit a few times and it'll go away."

"Of course it will go away," the girl says. "You're spitting it out."

But the girl has no response when, while standing in line for the Liberty Bell, Marcus cups his hand to his head like a visor and says, "When the Russians nuke us, don't just close your eyes. You gotta cover them with your hands too, or else the blast will burn right through your eyelids." He demonstrates for them.

The girl says, "That's not going to happen."

Marcus spits on the sidewalk. "It's inevitable."

Later, a tour guide invites their group to gather around the Liberty Bell as she tells them the fascinating story of this remarkable piece of American history. Marcus laughs. "That's not even the real one," he says. "It's a fake. The real one split in two."

"They fixed it," the girl says.

"That's why there's the crack?" the boy volunteers.

"They made the crack," Marcus says. "It's fake too." Then, "Everybody knows that."

———

THEY'VE STOPPED going to mass. It's been weeks, a month and a half maybe. Summer encloses them within its shapeless, secular human embrace. At first the boy feels thankful, relieved, but soon that passes and he feels guilty. Not guilty enough to want to return to mass, but guilty enough to feel bad about not going. You can never really escape, the boy thinks.

———

THE CHILDREN spend their first weekend at their father's apartment without Sarah. Where is Sarah? The father tells them Sarah said she was sorry, but she has to catch up on her schoolwork. She's been getting behind with her schoolwork this summer, he explains. She has two incompletes she needs to finish by the fall, and she doesn't know if she can get an extension.

"What's an extension?" the boy asks. The father explains what an extension is.

"What's an incomplete?" the girl asks, and the father explains that too, an idea so foreign, so strange, so mind blowing that it takes the girl a minute to grasp it. A placeholder grade. A temporary pass. Imagine putting off your report card until next year, having the whole summer to finish the work you should have finished during the school year—a dizzying notion. The girl wishes Sarah were there so the two of them could talk about Sarah's incompletes. Maybe the girl could help her—not with the assignments, but maybe some of the smaller tasks, like sharpening pencils or bookmarking pages or, well, anything Sarah might need. The girl is good at helping out, even if her mother never lets her help out with the mother's homework. The mother prefers solitude, the kitchen table her workstation, her island, her glowering fiefdom of isolated drudgery. Still, the girl arranges her mother's pens into neat rows and stacks her textbooks from largest to smallest, titles facing out, toward the kitchen entranceway.

They go to the pool with their father, but it's not the same. Their father prefers the shade and so chooses the lounge chairs beneath the cabana, where he can't see the girl execute a backflip or the boy dive into the deep end. Their father forgets the girl's goggles, forgets snacks. Their father forgets to bring them each a dry, oversized T-shirt to put over their bathing suits, so the children shiver in the post-swimming breeze that seems to double the moment the children step from the deep-end ladder and hug themselves all the way back to the cabana, their feet leaving semicolon shaped prints that diminish to commas by the time their father hands them a towel.

"You two ready?" he asks.

For lunch they eat their father's sandwiches, bologna and

cheese but without the tomatoes, avocados, and romaine lettuce that Sarah adds. The girl finishes hers without tasting a thing. The boy is happy to get extra Pringles, a no-no in Sarah's book.

––––––––

AS MUCH AS you long for solitude, the father thinks, the moment you get it, you don't know what to do with it. A weekend without the children, without Sarah, offers up so many pleasures—sleeping in, listening to music, walking to the corner store to get the Sunday *Times*, just like in college—that the father can't enjoy a single one of them. Friday night, he drinks too much, and the drinks wash his dreams onto strange shores. Twice, he wakes to a car alarm sounding in the parking lot; another time, a rat nibbling on cellophane is revealed, in the sudden nimbus of light from his bedside lamp, to be a piece of wrapping paper caught in the ceiling fan's breeze.

In the morning, the father decides to get up and get his day started, which seems permission enough to lie in bed for another forty minutes. He tries listening to music, but more and more, music is little more than nostalgia, the point of listening to music not to listen to music, but to listen to music *again*. The father turns the music off. He doesn't really want the *Times* but puts his shoes on anyway, finds his keys, wallet. Outside, someone has already started the day for him. He can hear children splashing in the pool and knows the sound should make him feel wistful for his own, but the only thing the sound makes him is grateful that he doesn't have to take the kids to the pool, a chore, a task, something else he's not terribly good at, something to add to making lunches, remembering suntan lotion, small talk, false cheer, staying married, and all the others.

He thinks about calling Sarah but doesn't.

"You'll call the minute you get lonely," Sarah said, the last time they were together. The father thought about protesting but couldn't think of what making a protest would be.

————

GUMMA CALLS. The girl answers.

"Heard your dad got dumped," she says. "That true?"

But the girl has already handed the phone to her brother, who is explaining, with a low degree of accuracy, what an incomplete grade is.

————

THE FATHER lets the children go to the pool by themselves. Tells them he'll join them in a little bit, he just has a few things he needs to catch up on.

"But," the boy protests, "by ourselves?"

"Other people will be there," the father says. "If you need something, just ask someone."

"But what about my suntan lotion?" the boy asks.

The father sighs, says it's time the boy learned how to do that for himself, isn't it?

"Duh, that's what I've been telling him this whole time," the girl says, but the girl has first-rate suntan lotion–applying skills, can rub it into a compliant translucence in a matter of seconds, while the boy always gets these pasty lakes across his arms and legs, with his sister yelling at him that he's using too much, does he know how much this stuff costs?

"I can't do it," the boy says, and begins to cry.

"Oh my God," the girl says, "you're such a baby."

"If you give me thirty minutes, I'll help you with it when I get there," the father says.

But thirty minutes yield to forty-five, and forty-five to fifty, while the boy shelters in the insufficient shade of a broken deck umbrella, its underside patterned with seahorses. After a while, his sister commands him to stand still while she angrily rubs lotion across his forehead, nose, cheeks, and shoulders. "It's so much easier if you just do it yourself," she sighs. "If you would just do it for yourself once, you'd see how much easier it is than having someone else do it."

The boy says, "Maybe I don't want to."

"Especially around the eyes," the girl says.

"Maybe I don't care," the boy says.

And the girl would have told him that that's what a baby would say, if she didn't notice, out of the corner of her eye, the bicycle man observing her from the pool fence. He's got something in his milk crate, either rags or shirts or towels, the girl can't tell. His hands grip the handlebars, like he's ready to go, but he's supporting his weight on one leg, taking a break, resting. Watching.

There's no end to the world's supply of menace, the girl thinks. All you have to do is look off to the side and there it is again, eyeing you while you had no idea.

ELEVEN

THE LAWN GETS so high the boy cannot get the mower through it. His mother tells him she'll hire someone as soon as all this rain passes, but all this rain does not pass; it only rains more. And more. So much rain. The lawn sends up fantastic weeds, white flowers the size of shoelace eyelets; a red-and-purple vine that clings to the underside of the air conditioning unit; pale mushrooms appear near the woodpile. The boy makes a game of clubbing them with a Wiffle ball bat. The boy is remarkably good at taking two mushrooms out with one powerful swing. Three, even. Amazing, what you can get good at.

When the rain passes, Alan and Chris appear, like abject rainbows. "Whew," Alan says, tossing the boy's football to himself. "Your lawn looks like a fucking jungle."

"Yeah!" Chris laughs, as if this were the funniest thing. "A jungle." He makes an ooh-ooh sound and swings his arms until the boy realizes this must be Chris's impersonation of a monkey.

"You know what they use in the jungle?" Alan says. "Machetes."

"You got any machetes?" Chris says.

"We have a weed thing," the boy says.

"A weed thing?" Chris says.

"It's like, a thing you hit weeds with," the boy explains.

"Go get it," Alan says.

The boy gets it. The weed thing: a strange marriage of golf club and scythe, a toothed blade, sharp to the touch.

"The weed thing," Chris says, and takes a few practice swings. "Nice."

"Here," Alan says, and Chris hands it to him. Alan places his hands around the weed thing's rubber grip, swings, and takes out a divot of grass the size of a backpack.

"Whoa!" Chris says.

"You can't do the whole yard with this," Alan explains, "but you could at least chop a path."

The boy considers this. "A path from where?"

"From here," Alan says, taking another monster swing. Grass flies, unevenly hacked. "To the porch."

"Yeah," Chris says, and then grabs the weed thing. "Like a snow path."

"But," the boy protests, but Chris is already on his next swing. When Chris swings, he raises the weed thing high above his head and brings it down with a thrilling whoosh—the boy never realized how exciting the weed thing could be, so many thanks to Alan and Chris on that. The way it passes through the grass like it isn't even there. The little whipping sound the grass sometimes makes. Chris tells them to back off; he doesn't want to hit them. "This thing could kill you," he says, enthusiastically. His face is flushed, hot.

"My turn," Alan says taking the weed thing from Chris. "Ew, gross. You got it all sweaty."

"I can't help it," Chris explains. "It's how my body functions."

A few swings later, the path is complete. Alan asks the boy, "You got any more of that lemonade you had last time?"

The boy says he doesn't think so. He would have to check.

"Bet I can find it," Alan says, and the boy tells him they're not supposed to have anyone in the house. But Alan says they'll just be in there for a minute, so it's not really like they're in the house; it's more like they're just visiting, right?

"Well," the boy says.

"Just visiting," Chris says. "Like in Monopoly."

"Well," the boy says.

Inside, the house is warm, the air conditioner on the fritz again. "Man," Chris says, "this place is a mess." And he's right: the kitchen table is covered with the mother's books and papers, each kitchen chair stacked high with bills, envelopes, and more papers, their ends curling in the humidity. Unwashed dishes rise from the sink, the dishwasher door swung wide, revealing more dishes stacked inside, two plates to a slot, the top shelf crammed with cups and mugs. Newspapers and pizza boxes cover the countertop, the ones the girl sometimes arranges into piles. "Where do you guys even eat?" Chris asks.

The boy tells him they eat in the family room.

"Man," Chris says, "you people need to do some serious cleaning."

"Quiet," Alan says, as he reaches into the refrigerator, grabs the lemonade pitcher, and take a long swallow straight from its spout. "Don't you know your manners?"

———

YOU WOULD think that watching your parent's marriage dissolve might prepare you for the end of your father's short-lived relationship with Sarah, but you would be wrong, the girl would have you know, because even though she's asked her father what happened to Sarah, and even though her father has weakly explained that the two of them are taking a break from each other while Sarah focuses on her schoolwork, the girl still does not understand. All she knows is that the next time she and her brother spend the weekend at their father's apartment, Sarah's stuff is gone, vanished, absent, like so many coins dropped into the father's old bank. The girl presses her father for more information until the father grows sullen, the way he does when the girl has him cornered. He tells her he knows as much as she does, which can't be true.

"That can't be true," the girl says, and, because the worst possible thing to do at that moment would be to cry, the girl begins to cry. The father tries to soothe her. That can't be true, the girl cries, over and over again. The father tells her he's sorry she's upset. Maybe they can talk about it more tomorrow when they're both not feeling so tired?

"That's what you always say," the girl cries. "But then we never do."

What is it exactly you are supposed to say when your young daughter has you dead to rights, your old moves now easy prey, slow-moving targets? That's what the father would like to know. How is a parent to parent, when one's parenting has lost something off its fastball? "Tomorrow," the father says, but honestly, he wouldn't believe him either.

———

THE NEXT TIME Gumma calls, she says she wants to talk to the girl. But the girl doesn't want to talk to Gumma, so the boy must talk to Gumma again since there's no one else for her to talk to. Another evening without a babysitter. Another night when the boy must soon put himself to bed and turn off the light.

To the boy, Gumma says, "Your mother was never a responsible person. Parenting has always been over her head."

The boy wants to say that isn't true, but Gumma says, "And your father never wanted to be a father in the first place."

"But," the boy says.

"Neither of them ever really wanted to be parents," Gumma continues, and then crunches an ice cube for a few seconds, which gives the boy permission to do something he's never thought to do before: he hangs up.

A PROBLEM: Cliff wants to spend the night. Solution: let Cliff spend the night on a weekend when the children are at their father's. Problem: what to do when Cliff wants to spend the night when the children are not at their father's? Solution: bill the event as a Marcus Sleepover! But will the children buy it? The mother cannot tell. She sets up Marcus in the guest bedroom, where her husband slept those last few weeks in the house. The room still holds his unhappy breath, or at least she needs to open the windows more often. There's little of her husband in this room really, save the ancient TV, a leftover from his bachelor days, too heavy and too outdated to move elsewhere. It's the first thing Marcus notices about this unremarkable room, though; he turns it on while the mother is explaining that he can put his things into the top dresser drawer, says, "I don't mind black-and-white like some people do. Sometimes I even like it better." The mother tells him that's good, recalls the times Gumma stayed with them, blaring Carson into the night, and thinks to say, "Just don't turn it on at night."

But Marcus does turn it on at night. The boy sneaks into the guest room to watch with him. The girl says she's going to tell, but she lingers too when Marcus adjusts the antenna to find the only station that isn't a "salt and pepper war," as Marcus puts it. Together, the three of them watch a commercial for aspirin. A construction worker takes a break from jackhammering a sidewalk to tell them that, after a long day on the job, the only thing that will cure his headache is Excedrin Extra. Because with Excedrin Extra, the construction worker gets enough headache relief to tackle even the toughest of jobs, like—and here, the commercial shows him sitting down to tea with his adorable, wide-eyed daughter and all her stuffed animals—making a special occasion truly special for a special someone. The worker fills a cup for a teddy bear wearing a hardhat and smiles.

"Those guys are all millionaires," Marcus says.

"Who?" the boy asks.

"Construction guys," Marcus says. "They make, like, a hundred dollars an hour."

"No they don't," the girl says.

Marcus shrugs. "Fine, don't believe me," he says, but the boy can tell his sister is on the fence. "But it's true. Lots of people who pretend to be poor are really rich." Marcus gives the two of them a look. "Your parents ever give the garbage men money for Christmas?"

The boy says, "Sometimes," even though he knows they always do.

"Well, don't," Marcus says. "Those guys make so much money already, it's crazy. That's like putting gravy on top of gravy. Those guys are laughing at you for giving them more money. Plus, they get to keep anything they want. Once you put your trash out on the curb, it belongs to them. Legally."

The girl sighs. "That's not true."

"Like I said," Marcus says, "don't believe me."

"Who told you all this?" the boy says.

"Nobody. It's common knowledge."

Common knowledge. A bright thread throughout Marcus's multicolored conversation. So many things are common knowledge; Marcus is merely a reporter, the children discover, merely wanting to pass along what is common knowledge to everyone else, so that they get up to speed. If you need to brush your teeth but forgot your toothpaste and toothbrush, you can clean your teeth by eating a slice of sandwich bread and your teeth will be even cleaner than with toothpaste, although dentists don't want you to know that, since their real job is to keep you brushing so that you'll buy lots of toothpaste and toothbrushes. That's how they make their money.

"But dentists don't sell toothbrushes and toothpaste," the girl points out. "They give you samples for *free*."

"Yup," Marcus says. "You ever wonder why those samples are so small? So you'll run out and have to buy more, that's why."

"Duh," the girl says. "That's why it's called a *sample*. That's what a sample is."

"Samples are a trick to make you buy more," Marcus says, with a satisfied click of his tongue. "Common knowledge."

And, weeks later, when the boy feels confident enough to show Marcus his secret collection of discarded cigarette lighters, Marcus says, "You can mix the fluid together to make a bomb."

"How?"

"Easy," Marcus says. "Common knowledge."

––––––

SHE'S LET some of her parenting go, is how the mother thinks of it. Just a little. She has to let go or else she'd go crazy trying to parent the way she used to, back in that era when parenting was wrapped up in her notion of home, household, family, self. Parenting is still on friendly terms with all of those, yes, but they don't hang out together nearly as often anymore. It's more like they sometimes see each other at parties, and it's fine for the most part, but kind of awkward too. Take the other day, for example. The mother was running the vacuum in her daughter's room because she hadn't run the vacuum for weeks and she knew Cliff would be coming over—strange, to think he would care—and those seemed reasons enough to get out the Electrolux and run a long attachment beneath her daughter's bed. She got on her knees to peer beneath the bed and saw the baton. The same marching baton her daughter kept beneath her bed since forever, the one the mother sometimes opened to read the notes hidden within. Notes she always felt were addressed to her, although the notes seemed directed to anyone who might be snooping. Still, the mother liked to read them, hieroglyphs to her daughter's personality, moods, dreams. But this time she did not open the baton. She did not read the old notes or the new ones, if there were any. She pushed the baton aside and vacuumed beneath the bed, and then replaced the baton just as she had found it. That she had no desire to read the notes was something she would rather not think about, so she did not think about it.

———

ALL THROUGHOUT the hottest part of summer, through every occasion the five of them share together—the mother, the children, Cliff, and Marcus—through every event, trip, meal, excursion, or celebration, Marcus makes it a point to stick a finger up his nose in photographs. A pose. He opens his eyes wide, his expression gleeful, his finger up his left nostril. A joke.

"Marcus, knock it off," Cliff says, but Marcus does not knock it off. He sticks his finger up his nose at Pappy's Pizza, outside Veteran's Stadium, on the family porch, in front of Cliff's birthday cake, at Lums Pond, while waiting for a parade, while eating a caramel apple, while modeling his new Philadelphia Fury T-shirt—photographs saved to the family album, where, years later, they strike the girl as a remarkable accomplishment, a sustained project, Marcus's fidelity to a bad joke a form of some kind of devotion.

———

EVEN THOUGH the boy is the only one to know it, the wasps are after him. They are. They've got it out for the boy, always have, from the time two summers ago when one stung him while he was playing on the back deck, a welt the size of a half dollar, to the time last summer when the boy put his hand beneath his pillow—his *pillow*! the very last word in domestic comfort, safety, and solace—and a wasp stung him on his palm. The boy's fingers had curled slightly, like a broken-in mitt, and itched, no matter how much lotion his mother administered. The boy slept with his hand atop his covers, afraid.

But this summer, the wasps have outdone themselves. Their plan: to build a nest atop the automatic garage door opener's chain, a muddy, ball-shaped nest that moves whenever the door is raised or closed, which isn't often, since as the wasps have clearly figured out, the family doesn't use the automatic opener as much as when their father was around: the mother parks in the driveway now. Cruel wasps, profiting from his parents' separation. The nest has a single opening at the bottom, like the Death Star's lone eye. Sometimes the boy sees wasps entering or leaving the opening, off to plan their next attack. Their legs drag lazily through the air like doomed kites. Their wings, striking the garage ceiling, make tiny buzzing noises. Whenever the boy must enter the garage, he runs to the door as quickly as possible and slams it behind him with the feeling of escape, a narrow miss.

"You could use a firecracker," Marcus says, when Marcus catches him running through the garage one day, and the boy must explain about the nest. "Just shove it in that hole, light it, and ka-blam! Sayonara wasps."

For a moment, the boy understands Marcus's life completely, grasps it as if it were his own, a world fitted out with problem-solving, bravery, and derring-do, where firecrackers are as ordinary and as easily obtained as birthday candles, but then the moment passes and the boy must figure out how to ask Marcus how they would find firecrackers, let alone light them off with their parents in the house, and it's like Marcus is someone he could never truly know.

———

THE MOTHER takes the girl to a doctor's appointment. The girl must get a physical exam before the school year starts, a requirement, the mother says, although she complains about having to take a vacation day—the only time the doctor had available—to drive her to the doctor's office. Inside the office, summer can find no purchase: a dark-paneled waiting room with heavy curtains drawn tight invites them to take a seat next to a coat stand strangely topped with knit caps and scarves. A lost and found, the girl thinks, but she doesn't care really; she must select enough magazines to keep her mother safely at bay. The girl decides on *Consumer Reports*, *Good Housekeeping*, *Reader's Digest*, and *Highlights*, just for old time's sake. The girl opens *Consumer Reports* and learns about microwave ovens. Turns out they're not all the same. It's all about the carousel. It's all about wattage. Programming options.

A few minutes later, a smiling nurse leads them to an exam room, asks the girl a few embarrassing questions, and then instructs the girl to remove her shoes and stand on a scale while the nurse finds the balance point, simultaneously writing down the results with a pen tethered to a clipboard. The nurse lowers a bar to the girl's head and tells her she's grown two inches since her last exam, how about that? The mother says that's really something, isn't it, and the girl smiles and knows she must agree, even though she senses those inches like something gone. How poorly her body knows her, the girl thinks. Always throwing a party without inviting her. The girl puts her shoes on with no memory of having taken them off.

Next, the girl and her mother wait in an examination room. The girl rests atop the exam table, a vinyl bed fitted with crinkly paper, and swings her legs idly, as she did when she was young. Two new inches, and nowhere to go. The exam door opens once to admit a mother and child who have wandered into the wrong room and later admits the child, alone, who looks at the girl as if the girl has misplaced the universe, until the girl says, "Wrong room," and the child closes the door on this lonely scene: a mother and daughter killing time, with nothing to say to one another. Should have invited the kid to stay. Anything to break this silence. The two of them are getting more and more used to this silence, they are, although the girl doesn't like to think about that. The problem is that the girl must avoid talking about Sarah, even if Sarah is on her mind. Her mother doesn't even know that Sarah has sort of moved out or moved on or whatever. In a way, the girl realizes, she's keeping Sarah from moving out by not telling her mom about it. Not that she would talk about Sarah with her mom anyway. Now the girl has the additional burden of not talking about Sarah to preserve Sarah, because, if she's honest with herself, the girl thinks, her mother would probably be happy to learn about Sarah's departure. Or whatever it is. The girl must now doubly not mention Sarah.

"Watch your legs," her mother says.

"My legs?"

"You keep swinging them."

The girl wants to deliver a killer shrug, but at that moment the door opens and the doctor enters the room with a rubber tomahawk she later uses to trick the girl's legs into kicking.

Afterward, the doctor asks the mother if it's all right if she and the girl have a talk together. Alone. The mother says fine, of course, tells the girl she'll wait for her in the waiting room, but not before giving the doctor a look the girl will later understand as conspiratorial. Once she's left, the doctor asks the girl a few questions unlike anything she's ever been asked before. Questions about her body, about some changes she might have noticed, about changes that are on the way. Things to look for, be aware of, keep in mind. The girl wants to tell the doctor she knows about all of these things—Judy Blume spoiled everything years ago—but finds herself nodding like a bumpkin anyway. The doctor counsels her that she'll need to be more aware of her body now, more aware of men too, and gives her some dubious-sounding advice about keeping her legs crossed in public, sitting up straight in restaurants, and refusing rides alone with men, even if she knows them. The girl thinks about the bicycle man watching her from the pool fence. The way he didn't look away when she returned his gaze. He'd done something she hadn't remembered until now, something the doctor's cautionary tale unwantedly retrieves from the wherever of her mind: he'd winked at her. Right before he pedaled away.

———

THE FRIEND wants to know how Cliff is in the sack, but the mother won't budge. "I would tell *you*," the friend says.

"You would," the mother agrees.

"I *have* told you."

The mother says, "You have."

———

THE NEXT TIME the babysitter babysits the children, he tells them to come outside. He has something to show them, he says. Something that's pretty much going to blow their minds, so they'd better hurry. The girl leaves the house in flip-flops; the boy goes barefoot. In the driveway, a Pontiac Firebird, brown, with a double white stripe down the side. "Well?" the babysitter says, and the children tell him it's cool.

"Cool?" the babysitter says. "Wait 'til you get inside it." He fumbles for his keys and opens the driver's side door, which makes a sudden creaking noise—"still working on that"—and tells the children to check it out. So the children check it out. For the boy, for whom cars don't really matter yet the way they seem to matter to other boys, the interior looks like a spaceship, shiny, with a Swiss cheese–patterned steering wheel, the holes big enough to put his fingers through. For the girl, who imagines herself as passenger, not driver, the seats look too low: sit down in them and you might as well be sitting on the floor. The children have never been asked to admire a car's interior before, an act as strange and unfamiliar as appraising wine, but the children know when to ooh and ah, and so they say appreciative things about the car. The girl says the seats look comfy. The boy thinks the steering wheel is neat.

"Come on," the babysitter says, opening the passenger door, "step inside my sweet ride."

Inside: a rich compound of cigarettes, pine-scented air freshener, Armor All, and the faint fustiness of unwashed clothes—the babysitter has left some laundry on the backseat. "Sorry about that," he says, "you can just scoot it over." The boy scoots it over; his sister takes the passenger seat. The babysitter gets behind the wheel, puts the keys in the ignition, and asks them if they are ready. The children say they are. The babysitter tells them it doesn't always start on the first try, and the children assure him that's fine, they understand, even though they cannot recall that ever happening with their parents' cars. "Here goes," the babysitter says, turning the key. The engine wakens, roars, and then, just as the babysitter flashes one of the happiest expressions the boy has ever seen on him, dies. "Hold on," the babysitter says, "let me pump it." The boy doesn't understand what that means, until the babysitter stomps the gas pedal like it's a bug he's trying to kill, and then that's one less thing the boy doesn't understand. Pump the pedal. The boy recalls Florida, the golf cart, the feeling of racing it down the golf course hill.

The car starts. The babysitter says he just needed to give it some gas, that's all, now check this out. He presses the pedal even harder and turns a devilish grin on them. "Hear that?" he says.

The children do; they hear that, as most of the neighborhood must too, the girl thinks.

"That's the sound of power," the babysitter says.

"Wow," the boy says.

The three of them sit in the driveway until the sound of power cuts out and leaves them with the sound of their driveway at night, a not-altogether-unpleasant tune, the boy thinks. "Gave it too much gas," the babysitter says. "Damn." He turns the radio on, loud, and shows the children how to work the knobs, how bass means low sounds, treble means high, how balance means left or right. The children nod, say, Oh, even though they already know about radios. Grown-ups, it's all a matter of giving them a little gas.

———

ONE NIGHT, the children are alone in the house, sans babysitter, their mother working late, as she does more often now, when they hear a knock at the door. Which is impossible, the boy thinks. No one knocks on their front door aside from Alan and Chris, and there's no way Alan and Chris are knocking at their front door on a Wednesday night at nine-thirty. Impossible. This, the boy's thought as someone knocks on the door again.

"Anybody home?" a voice says. A man's voice.

"Please," a second voice says. A woman. "We need help."

The boy feels something happening in his legs. This thing where neither one wants to commit to keeping him upright all of a sudden. You do it, one leg tells the other; no, *you*. Somehow, the boy walks to the kitchen, where his intention reveals itself to him: grab the biggest kitchen knife you can find.

"What are you doing?" the girl says. She's just come from the family room, watching the shows she watches whenever they're alone at night. Gumma shows. Shows where everyone walks around smoking cigarettes while wearing a damp bath towel. "Put that down!"

The boy puts the knife down. "Don't answer it."

"Don't be stupid," the girl says.

"Please!" the boy says, feeling himself begin to cry. For he knows something his sister does not, something he cannot explain or make her understand: it's those two teenagers at their front door. The ones who died in the car crash. The ones who were looking at the fence, the way it gets all blurry when you tilt your head to the side.

But the girl is already at the front door. Says, "Who's there?" with an authority the boy didn't know she had. As good as anything their mother could summon.

"We need a phone," the woman says. "Please."

"If you tell me the number, I can call," the girl says. She's sharp sometimes, the boy has to admit it. Never would have thought of that himself.

"We had an accident," the woman says. "Please."

"OK," the girl says, "but we've got a dog in the basement. Just so you know."

"OK," the woman says.

"Big dog," the boy says. The girl shoots him a look.

"Please," the woman says.

The girl opens the door. A woman, not much older than the babysitter's girlfriend, closer to Sarah's age perhaps, steps inside, says thanks, while her boyfriend, bare-chested and barefoot, yet inexplicably wearing an orange knit cap in the middle of summer, stumbles in behind her, his hand clutching what the boy realizes is a crumpled-up map to his forehead, the map damp with blood. "We hit a tree," the man explains. His breath exudes the smell of smoke. His chest is slick with sweat.

"May we please use your telephone?" the woman says with strange formality, although her words are slurred and her hair is wild, windblown. She's wearing the shortest shorts the boy has ever seen.

"We need to call Dee-Dee," the man explains.

The woman groans. "You're not calling Dee-Dee."

"I'll call Dee-Dee if I want to," the man says, then removes the map from his eye. His eye is swollen shut.

"This is just like the time with the boat," the woman says.

The man regards the bloody map as if it might tell him something. What is this place? Where am I? "Don't bring up the boat."

"You and Dee-Dee," the woman says, "and that stupid boat."

The man returns the map to his eye. "I just said don't bring up the boat."

A few moments later, the woman makes a phone call while the man slumps in one of the kitchen chairs, his head on the table, which is covered with envelopes and bills. Going to get blood on those, the boy thinks. What will their mother say? The girl brings the man and woman two glasses of ice water. The four of them sit in the nimbus of light from the kitchen fixture, an inverted bowl etched with leaves. The woman tells the man to get his head off the table. The man says his head wasn't on the table. Eventually, a car rumbles down the driveway, idles noisily, then sounds its horn.

"Dee-Dee," the man says.

After they've left, the girl cleans the front doorknob, entrance-way, kitchen table, kitchen chairs, and the telephone receiver with

Windex and paper towels. Then she pulls the kitchen bag from the trash and tosses it into the garage trash can, covering her tracks. When the girl swears the boy to secrecy—that they will never tell their mother, ever, no matter what—the boy can't believe how easily he agrees.

TWELVE

ONE WEEKEND, the children return from their father's house to discover that Cliff is already there, moved in, it seems, although their mother says the move is temporary. She tells them Cliff only needs a place to stay while he and his ex-wife sell their old house — Marcus's house — which shouldn't take too long. Besides, Cliff won't be around much since he works during the week like her, but unlike her has to work occasional weekends too. The thing the children need to know is that Cliff feels as awkward about staying in the house as the children feel about him staying there, so what do you say we make a nice effort to make him feel at home, the mother says, and then realizes she's smiling her cheerleader smile, the one that only works on the boy anymore. The girl sighs, says, "Why does he have to live *here*?" and the mother is about to answer when the boy asks, "What about Marcus?" a question she'd much rather answer, and so chooses to answer it.

"He's at his mother's for now, but he'll stay here sometimes too." Oh, that smile, is it widening? It is, her daughter's expression informs her, it is. "Won't that be fun?" Ugh.

"I thought you said it was temporary," the girl says.

"It is," the mother says, "temporary. At least up until the school year begins."

"What? That's like, four weeks from now!" the girl says.

"Three and a half," the mother says. "But maybe sooner. That's what temporary means."

The girl snorts. "I know what temporary means." She walks

away, heads upstairs, even as the mother calls her name, a ritual the boy is getting more and more familiar with. The boy knows what temporary means too, but even so, he's not sure what to make of Cliff's unnatural presence in their home, no matter how kind Cliff is (he never uses the TV), how quiet he seems (sometimes the boy thinks he's alone in the house only to discover Cliff standing on the back deck watching the evening sky), or how deferential he is to the children (he asks them if he may use the telephone). Cliff is fastidious. Cliff rearranges the linen closet to maximize efficiency, fixes the boy's fan on the sly so that it no longer squeaks, folds laundry so quickly that it's still warm from the dryer by the time the girl retrieves it from the basket. Once, the children are eating ice cream in front of the TV when Cliff asks them what's that on top?

"Magic Shell," the boy says.

"Magic Shell?"

The mother explains Magic Shell to Cliff. "Oh," Cliff says. "Where is it?"

"In the fridge," the mother says.

A moment later, Cliff returns with the bottle of Magic Shell, reading its ingredients aloud. "Do you know what's in this stuff?" he says, and then reads a list of polysyllabic preservatives. "I don't even know what half these things are."

The children say they don't either; they just eat it.

"Oh, all right," Cliff says, as if something has been settled. A moment later, he returns to the family room with a giant bowl of vanilla ice cream, shellacked with a heavy, glossy coating of Magic Shell.

"Cliff," the mother says.

"You have to let it get dry first," the boy instructs.

But Cliff is already on his second spoonful. "So good," he says.

WHAT'S BETTER than setting things on fire at home? Setting things on fire outside the home, of course. Marcus has only been in the house less than a week, and already he knows about a place they can go to light some serious fires. The perfect place. "I'll show you if you promise not to blab your little face off," he tells the boy.

"I promise not to blab my little face off," the boy says, which the boy didn't even realize was funny until Marcus's creepy laugh, a series of deep snorts mottled with complete silence, lets him in on it.

Marcus leads him through the neighborhood and out to the road the boy's bus takes. The boy knows the road well enough, but only from bus-level, which didn't tell him, he realizes now, how much litter actually lines the shoulder or how malodorous the asphalt gets at this time of day, the sun shimmering off its unlovely surface. Ragweed turns in the breeze, wearing white butterflies. The boy struggles to keep up with Marcus, flicks his lighter on the sly, hides it when cars pass by. They're walking toward the curve where the two teenagers were killed, the part of the road near the soccer fields where the fence does its trick, a fact the boy realizes he shouldn't share with Marcus the moment after he shares it with Marcus.

"Stupid teenagers," Marcus says, then spits a glob of saliva onto the road. "Probably drunk."

They reach their destination, the perfect place: the stream that borders the road on the opposite side of the soccer fields. The one the boy can see from the bus, a lazy waterway of no distinction whatsoever, save the sandy outcropping that stretches to its middle, accessible by jumping a backwater fen the approximate width of a twin bed. Even the boy can make that jump, Marcus says, and the boy nearly does, one semisoaked Ked notwith-standing.

"Our private island," Marcus says.

"Yeah," the boy says.

"Fire Island."

"Yeah. Fire Island."

"Don't repeat what I say," Marcus says. "Makes you sound stupid."

The boy mumbles something that's a loose composite of sorry and OK and why. A moment later, Marcus orders the boy to collect some sticks while he gets to work on a firepit, which turns out to mean a giant hole Marcus digs by kicking the ground with the heel of his Converse while the boy struggles to find any sticks that aren't currently employed as branches. His search informs him that they're still in view of the road; the boy watches a station wagon as it slows down to see what these two boys are up to, no good, no doubt. When the boy returns with three or four sticks he found half-submerged in the stream, Marcus has already taken the lighter to a pile of leaves, which refuse to burn.

"What the hell are these supposed to be?" Marcus says.

"Sticks?"

"We need dry sticks, dumbass," Marcus says, knocking the sticks from his hands.

"But you said sticks?"

"Are you really that stupid?" Marcus says. "Jesus." And then Marcus goes into a speech the boy will turn over in his mind again and again, despite his attempts not to, despite his promises to himself that he will forget everything Marcus said that day at Fire Island. How the boy is an idiot, he really is, and is it any wonder his sister can't stand him and his daddy moved away and shacked up with a new girlfriend and his momma wants a divorced daddy for a boyfriend, anything to get away from him and all of his stupidity?

Eventually, the leaves catch fire.

———

THE GIRL has a plan how she can see Sarah again, but the plan involves tricking her mother into driving her to Sarah's restaurant without her mother's realizing it, sans her brother, who will give everything away, also while somehow ditching her mom at the restaurant so that she won't know what she's up to either. An unlikely, unworkable plan; but still—how to make it work? Lies, the girl thinks. Lies, those great problem-solvers. She could tell her mother she forgot something at the restaurant. A jacket? No, it's summer. She couldn't possibly leave an item of clothing. A notebook? A notebook of what? A notebook for school. But school is out, so no notebook. But something school-related would be good. One of her summer reading books? Not bad, but her mother knows she got most of her summer reading books at the library, already returned, shelved. Right. Hmm. Well, her mom doesn't know her father got her one of the books (this is true, although the girl hasn't even started it yet, the book marooned with the other few possessions she keeps at her father's apartment), which would give her the perfect option: a lie that's got just a little bit of truth in it. The best kind of lie, the girl has learned, no stranger to non-truths, this girl is, from time to time, of course.

"You left your summer reading book at a restaurant?" her mother says. "How did that happen?"

The girl explains that she brought it to the restaurant to read since she hates waiting around for her dad to finish his coffee after dessert, which always takes forever, and she must have put it down on the seat, or maybe it fell on the floor, she doesn't know. "Maybe we could go check to see if it's there?" the girl says, adding a necessary lie, "I'm supposed to write a book report on it."

So, off to the restaurant the three of them go, the boy's mouth shut under penalty of the girl's telling their mother about his cigarette lighter collection, the girl rehearsing what she will say when her mother pulls into a parking space —*I'll just run inside and ask*— when her mother, not privy to the girl's rehearsal, brings the car to a stop in the same space the father used the first time the children met Sarah, in that early era of separation, and says, "I'll get it."

"No," the girl protests, "I can do it."

"Then do it fast," the mother says. "I don't want to sit here and bake in this hot car."

"Maybe we could all go," the boy volunteers, unhelpfully. "To stay cool?"

"Fine," the mother says.

"But it's *my* book!" the girl says, betraying her anxiety. A poorly played hand. "I should be the one to get it."

"But it's hot in here," the boy says.

"I'll be right back," the girl says.

"You take forever for *everything*," the boy says, not without accuracy. The girl's morning ablutions now clock in at nearly an hour. "You're a slowpoke."

"Shut up!"

"Enough," the mother says, then steps from the car. "Everybody out."

"But—"

"Everybody out of this stupid hot car before I lose my mind," the mother says, slamming her door.

They enter the restaurant, where someone has turned off most of the available air—the girl can feel it. At this hour, the restaurant is idle, nearly empty. The only diners the girl can see are two grandparent types stabbing two whipped-cream-heavy sundaes with spoons the length of knitting needles. From somewhere, a TV plays an afternoon talk show. The girl follows her mother to the register, where a non-Sarah hostess listens to her mother's query, frowns, draws her lips together in a manner Sarah never would, and says, "I can check lost and found for you. But I don't think I've seen anything like that."

"Thank you," the mother says, and non-Sarah disappears into the wherever behind the register and reappears a few moments later carrying a cardboard box. "You won't believe it," she says, with more accuracy than the girl will ever be able to let her know, "but I think you're in luck." She places the box beside the register and pulls out a copy of the book the girl lied to her mother about. "Is this it?"

"That's it," the mother says.

Non-Sarah hands the book to the girl. "Good thing you stopped by."

"Yeah," the girl says, turning the book over in her hands, a cheap, top-stained paperback torn at the edges that's probably been in the lost and found forever. "Good thing."

On the ride home, the girl watches cars, trees, and homes pass by like she's a visitor to an alien planet, the world a mystery, offering up one more impossibility after another.

————

ONE AFTERNOON, the boy's mother asks him to get a folding chair from the basement. The boy protests, but it's no use. Unlike his sister, the boy has no moves against his mother; he's never won an argument with her, never come close really. So, to the basement he goes. He descends the basement stairs, damp this time of year, slick with August humidity, and finds the light switch like always, a lone string hanging from a single bulb that illuminates the basement the instant before it goes out—pop! a burned bulb—a nano-second, but long enough for the boy to spot one of the Smash Up Derby cars lying upside down against a far wall. Still there. The boy has spotted it before, as his sister must have too, and has never moved it, as his sister must never have too.

———

WHY WOULD the father take the children on a hike? Who knows, but there he is at the state park, the children ahead of him, the boy in the lead, the girl turning her head from time to time to make sure he's keeping up. The father is not a hiker. The father wears boat shoes and dress socks. The father collects rocks along the path when the children aren't looking and then tosses them into the nearby woods, says, "Did you hear that? Probably a bear."

"Dad," the girl sighs. "It's just you throwing a rock."

"It is?"

"Yes."

"How can you be sure?"

"I'm sure."

"Well, I'm not so sure," the father says, and then tosses another rock in plain view. "Good thing I have these rocks to protect us."

The boy walks ahead. He isn't certain whether he should be trying to look at everything around him or just focus on his feet, which seems easier to do; the boy is good at navigating roots, rocks, slippery grasses, mud, leaves, ankle-threatening holes. You can't always look around at nature. You have to look down, at least a little. The boy watches the trail pass beneath his feet. Nature is many things, the boy decides, but mostly it's really repetitive.

———

WHEN THE CHILDREN return from their father's, their mother says she has something to tell them and then begins to cry. Their grandfather has died. Heart attack. Yesterday. Their mother says she didn't want to tell them until they got back home from their father's, wanted to wait and tell them in person, she's so sorry. The girl cries and hugs her mother, says, Oh, Mom. The boy doesn't quite cry but feels a funny sort of feeling in his throat and eyes and hugs his mother too. Standing in the kitchen, the girl's and mother's individual cries veering toward the communal, it occurs to the boy that the three of them haven't spent time like this together in a while.

A decision must be made: will the children attend the funeral? The mother says she will leave it to them. She tells the children they are both old enough to go or not go, should they choose not to go. They shouldn't feel bad if they choose not to go. Everyone will understand if they choose not to go. No one will be angry or upset in the least, if they choose not to go. Absolutely not. That's something she wants them to understand, OK? When she says this, though, she looks more at the boy than she looks at the girl, and the boy gets the feeling she's really only talking to him. Combine that with the decision that was already shaping up in the boy's head, that he would choose not to go, and it's like he's not really even making a decision at all when he says, "I think I won't go, Mom," and his mom cries a little more and says, "It's OK, sweetie," and pulls him close.

The girl, however, decides to go, and, as much as the boy feels he's made the right decision, the girl feels she's made the right choice too, knows it the moment her mother looks at her and whispers thanks so quietly the boy can't hear. And, just like that, the decision has been made, such an easy thing really. Now, the hard part: attending her grandfather's funeral, which, the girl realizes as soon as she's registered her mother's approval, she doesn't really want to attend, she only wanted to make her mother happy, because why would she want to attend a funeral, and why oh why didn't she just take an easy pass, like her brother? See him standing there, thinking his thoughts all to himself, the coward, the scaredy-cat, the big baby. The winner.

The day of the funeral, the boy stays home with Cliff, while the girl and her mother chaperone the grandmother to the church, where a mass intrusively asserts itself, one large, silver casket opened to reveal the grandfather's unnatural, overdressed body notwithstanding. First impressions of a dead body: death looks a lot like sleeping, but not quite, either. The girl accompanies her mother to casket, kneels with her, and says a prayer, without crying. They've placed the grandfather's hands atop his chest in a way the girl cannot imagine the grandfather placing his hands, his stiff shirtsleeves studded with cufflinks, something else the girl cannot recall him wearing. His face appears dimly beneath the one death has imposed atop it, his expression slyly pleased, as if he's just recalled a tune he's been trying to place all day. Someone has cropped his fingernails.

The girl receives the consolations of family, friends, relatives she hasn't seen in ages. "We're so sorry, sweetheart," these kind folks wish her to know, or, "How is your mom holding up?" followed by, "How are *you* holding up?" The girl tells them she is sad, but fine, her mom is doing fine, ends up saying this to so many people that she begins to understand something she did not understand at first, that as much as her relatives genuinely care about her and her feelings when they ask, "How is your mom holding up?" and "How are you holding up?" they don't only mean her grandfather's death, they mean her parents' separation. They feel sorry for her. They fear her a little too, in a way they didn't before the separation, knowledge the girl would rather not have.

And, as if today's funeral didn't break enough new ground, the girl has no idea what to do when her father shows up. She didn't even know he was coming, but there he is, wearing a dark suit and a dark expression, neither familiar to the girl. Her father says hello to a few relatives, gives the grandmother a hug, then gives her mother a hug, says something consoling to her, and then goes to kneel at the casket. It is the first time the girl has seen her father hug her mother since the separation. In a moment he will rise, walk over and give her a hug too—the girl can see that moment shaping up now—but not before the girl realizes something she didn't know she's realized for some time now but didn't want to accept: her parents will never get back together again. Ever. That's not going to happen. The separation will lead to divorce, which will lead to forever. Her parents' marriage is over and it's not coming back, and how often do we have no idea what's around the corner.

"It's OK, sweetie," her father says, the moment after everyone has turned to see the girl's sudden outburst of emotion. The girl can feel her father's arms around her and knows that she is crying, weeping, her chest heaving, but no one knows what she is crying about, and even if they did, they expected her to cry, given the situation, given everything. She's that kind of girl for them now.

———

WHAT DOES THE boy do the day of his grandfather's funeral? Learn chess, from Cliff, who, it turns out, is an excellent teacher, patient with the boy, good at explaining options, moves, strategy. The two of them sit at the kitchen table, the mother's piles of mail pushed aside. It is the boy's turn. He moves a pawn up a side rank. His plan: liberate the rook and let it go to town.

"Hmm," Cliff says. "Maybe try the middle instead."

"The middle?"

"Work the middle of the board," Cliff suggests, "save the sides for later."

The boy takes back his original move and instead moves a different pawn up one of the center ranks.

"Aha," Cliff says.

———

THE MOTHER has not gotten around to framing the girl's still life, a Mother's Day gift, like the Mother's Day painting she received last year and the one she received the year before that. This one isn't the girl's best, the mother thinks, something is off with the grapes, or are they cherries? The girl has signed the bottom corner, her signature more grown-up looking now, could be mistaken for an adult's, unlike the boy's, whose scribble dooms him to the playground, the sandbox, the shallow end, the children's menu. Grapes, the mother decides. Red grapes.

———

ONE AFTERNOON, when the boys are alone, Marcus inserts a firecracker into the wasps' nest, lights the fuse, and runs toward the garage door, where the boy is standing, waiting for him behind the half-closed door, the door only a door for few seconds, until the fuse reaches the firecracker, and the door becomes a shield.

After: the nest vanishes, gone.

After: three dead wasps lie in a circle on the garage floor, like someone has arranged them just so.

But not before the remnants of the nest catch fire. A fire that smolders atop the automatic garage door chain and threatens to catch the garage ceiling on fire. The boy's knees go loose; he feels himself beginning to cry. "It's on fire!" he says, but Marcus tells him to shut his stupid mouth, then drags the garden hose inside the garage and extinguishes the fire in an instant.

"You need to stop being a baby," Marcus says, and then instructs the boy to put the hose away and sweep the garage with the push broom until their tracks are covered.

Later, when the mother pulls her car into the garage and closes the door behind her without noticing what's happened, the boy can't decide whether he feels elated or disappointed. Is it possible to feel both?

———

THE MOTHER tells the friend things are going well with Cliff, for the most part.

"For the most part?"

"Right," the mother says, "except for the things that aren't."

"Like what?"

The mother considers this. She imagines Cliff standing before her, kind Cliff, quiet Cliff, with his hands in his pockets, rocking on his feet the way he sometimes does. Imaginary Cliff wants to know the answer too, so that he can correct the things that aren't going well. "Oh, the usual," the mother says.

"Quit stonewalling," the friend says. "I want details."

"I don't have details," the mother says, even though she knows this isn't entirely true. She has details, but they're all wrapped up in her worries, fears, and doubts, difficult to sort out. "Just feelings. You know those feelings you have when you realize things aren't probably going to work out, but you tell yourself you can overcome them anyway, if you try, and maybe that's all anyone else in a relationship does too, but trying seems like such an effort, and then you wonder whether the effort is worth it, or whether you'd be better off using that effort to close up shop instead, or whether the best possibility is to make no effort whatsoever and hope the other person doesn't notice that you've stopped making an effort a while ago, long enough, at least, until you can figure some painless way to get out of this whole thing. Do you know what I mean?"

After a significant pause, in which the mother can hear her friend's TV murmuring in the background, the friend says, "You've just described the past five years of my marriage."

———

THIS TIME they're going to do Fire Island the right way, Marcus says. No more searching around for sticks and branches and leaves that barely even catch fire; that's what a rookie would do, a greenhorn, a loser. What you've got to do is be prepared. Just ask the Boy Scouts, they've got it right on that front, even if the Boy Scouts are really a socialist plot to make you happy with losing your individuality and never wanting to do anything that everyone else wouldn't want to do too.

"What's a socialist?" the boy asks.

Marcus says, "You never heard of that? A socialist is the kind of a person who can't eat a meal unless somebody else had to pay for it first."

The boy considers this. "You mean like, a Happy Meal?"

Marcus snorts, tells the boy he's doesn't know the first thing. "Happy Meals are a marketing scheme to get kids hooked on McDonald's. Same thing as Ronald McDonald and Mayor Mc-Cheese."

The boy wants to ask what a marketing scheme is but instead says, "Even Grimace?"

Marcus lets out a low whistle. "Oh, yeah," he says, "you better believe Grimace is in on it too. Don't fall for his fat purple face. He's out to seduce you."

This time they've come to Fire Island prepared. The boy carries a plastic grocery bag, heavy with old newspapers, while Marcus' dons an out-of-season windbreaker, its ample pockets concealing lighters, matches, and a fresh bottle of lighter fluid, a gift, really, from Cliff, who has taken to grilling of late and to not noticing

Marcus's shenanigans for longer. They reach the firepit, still there, almost, despite one side's having collapsed in their absence: Marcus corrects this in an instant, falls to his knees, and begins scooping sand with his fingers. The boy, uncertain what to do, squats beside Marcus, opens the grocery bag, and takes the newspapers out. Folds a few in half, then folds the halves into quarters, presses them nice and neat.

"What the hell are you doing?" Marcus says.

"Making them flat?"

"Why the hell would you do that?" Marcus says, grabbing the newspapers from the boy's hands. "Fire needs air. Oxygen. Everybody knows that." Marcus unfolds a piece of newspaper and then crumbles it into a loose ball. "See? Like that."

"But it's coming apart?"

"That's the whole point," Marcus says, then tells the boy not to touch anything; he'll do the rest. "It's amazing how stupid you are sometimes."

"Am not," the boy says.

"No common sense," Marcus says. "That's your problem. That's the whole country's problem. Ever wonder why the country is in the shape it's in?"

"No."

"Course not," Marcus laughs, then begins tossing the crumpled newspaper into the firepit. "Why am I not surprised."

After Marcus has filled the firepit with crumpled newspaper and secured it in place with three or four medium-to-heavy logs the boy carried from the roadside, across the jump, and to the island, he tells the boy to check this out. Pulls the lighter fluid from the windbreaker pocket, unscrews the top, and squirts the fluid over the crumpled paper and logs. "That'll burn," Marcus says, and the boy can't help it; he gets excited.

"Yeah, that'll burn!" he says, louder than he intended.

Marcus turns to the boy and does something he hasn't done before: he slaps him, hard, on the back of the neck. "I told you not to repeat me," he says.

The boy, holding back tears, says he's sorry.

"It's like I have to tell you everything ten times," Marcus says. "Jesus. Now look what you made me do; you made me go and hit you."

The boy says he's sorry.

"I don't want to be the bad guy, so don't go making me one, OK?"

The boy says he won't.

"OK," Marcus says, the moment before he strikes the lighter and sets the flame to the newspapers, which burst into fantastic, blue-orange fireballs and begin to float like reverse snowflakes, up from the firepit and into the trees, intending harm, malice. They smolder and smoke, the wind carrying them wherever. The boy eyes one as it drifts toward the road, then sees a car pull over to the shoulder. A green hatchback with its windows down. A man wearing glasses and a long-sleeved dress shirt sits behind the wheel. His expression is hard to read, aside from anger, which becomes more legible the moment he steps from the car, slams the door, and shouts, "What the hell are you kids doing?" The man puts his hand to his eyes, shading them from the sun. "Just what the hell do you two kids think you're doing?" he says, but Marcus has already fled the island, his feet kicking up sand and water, and the boy has no idea how to answer the man's question.

THIRTEEN

THE CHILDREN have a secret they don't even know is a secret on account of each of them never sharing it with the other, but the fact of the matter is the two of them are kind of looking forward to the school year starting up again, since that will mean they won't have to spend so many weekends at their father's apartment, the way they do now. Staying at the apartment isn't the same since Sarah left, but neither of the children would ever say that to the other, even though they can guess the other probably feels the same way. That's how it is when you have a brother or sister and your parents split up and your father moves out; you can guess the other's feelings most of the time. Except for when you can't, and then it's like it used to be.

————

YOU KNOW, the father imagines Sarah saying, I don't like being a part of these imaginary conversations. I didn't when we were together, and now that were apart, it's—

Creepy? the father supplies.

Creepy, plus weird. Borderline pathetic.

I can live with borderline, the father muses.

Borderline, Sarah snorts. That's you, isn't it? Borderline something bordering on borderline something else.

But I was thinking—

You were thinking how you've never truly been alone until now, etc., etc., how this is the longest you've been alone since the summer after high school when your parents went to England and left you behind — wah! Poor you! — even though you didn't want to go, as you know, and took every opportunity to get out of going until your poor parents finally gave up and headed off across the pond, sans son, their little solo act, staying home in his lonely loneliness.

Right. I was eighteen.

That seems to impress you, that you were eighteen and alone for the first time. Which is strange since it's really sort of old, right? I mean, for being alone.

I led a sheltered life.

Jesus. Do you ever get tired of repeating the same phrases in your head? *A sheltered life.* That's another big one for you, that idea. You love that idea, don't you?

More like the truth than an idea.

Hmm, well, more like a truth-flavored idea. Or an idea brought to you by the same people who brought you truth. If you like truth, try this idea!

I haven't been truly alone since the summer I was eighteen.

See what I mean? You're stuck again.

Which means I haven't ever truly been alone as an adult.

Eighteen is an adult. Check the fine print.

Which means this is the first time I've truly been alone as an adult in my life. A new experience. The unknown.

Did I mention the thing about your being stuck on the same thought? And how that thought wasn't necessarily on the friendliest terms with anything we might call accuracy?

There's value in the experience of being alone.

Oh God.

That's something my loneliness is helping me see.

How thoughtful. You should send it a card.

I want to let loneliness lead me for a while and see where it goes.

To you drunk dialing me in about three nights from now, I'm guessing.

I want to open myself up to loneliness. To its offer of contemplation, solitude. Quiet. I'm willing to follow.

OK, but my money is on the drunk-dialing thing.

———

WHAT MARCUS wants to know is what's up with this bank? Marcus is in the boy's room again, his attention wandering from the chessboard the boy has painstakingly set up atop his bedspread. In the past few weeks, the boy has caught a major case of chess fever, but Marcus remains immune, the game too slow, too dull, too lame, he says, too full of waiting around for the other player to do something they could have just done five minutes ago without making everybody wait around like all everybody has is all the time in the world. *All the time in the world*, the boy thinks, and realizes that's what he loves best about the game, its casual offer of eternity.

"It's a bank," the boy says. Then, "My dad's."

Marcus inspects the bank, shakes it. "What's wrong with it?"

The boy explains how the bank works.

"What a stupid bank," Marcus says. "No wonder your dad wanted to get rid of it."

"No," the boy says, "he loves that bank."

"Not really," Marcus says, in that maddening way Marcus has of saying something as if it couldn't be any other way, unlike the boy, whose voice is already starting to betray his emotions when he says, "It was his first material possession."

"Six seventy-five," Marcus says. "That's nothing. You can't buy anything with that."

"When it gets to ten dollars?" the boy says.

"Ten dollars isn't anything anymore," Marcus says. He shakes the bank again, turns it upside down, and tries opening the door with his dirty fingers. "I bet when your dad was a kid, he thought ten dollars was a lot, but ten dollars isn't diddly-squat these days."

"It teaches you?" the boy says. "To save your money?"

But Marcus has already set the bank atop the chessboard, which buckles in at the center crease and sends the front-rank pieces rolling on their sides. "In a few years, we won't even have coins anymore," Marcus says. "Everything will be on credit cards. You watch."

———

CLIFF LIVING in the house with them. Well, the mother has made worse decisions, right? At some point? Even if she can't think of one offhand, that doesn't mean anything really, because this is a decision that will resolve itself. In a matter of weeks, Cliff will move out. There. Bad decision redeemed by passing time, wherein everyone gradually forgets original decision. Until then, make do, smile, one eye toward the calendar, August winding down, like Cliff's stay. And, while smilingly making do, it isn't as if Cliff's presence in the house bothers anyone else nearly as much as it bothers her, her daughter's sullen moodiness notwithstanding. Hard to escape that, though. Her daughter disapproves of Cliff to the same degree she seems to approve of her father's fling — or former fling, or whatever she was. Normally, the mother would feel angry about it, her daughter's easy loan of love and understanding to a woman who's logged as many parenting miles as moon orbits, but something tells the mother to let it pass or lose even more ground to her ex, whose stock seems to be plummeting lately, something she isn't too principled to take advantage of. We take what we can, when we can take it.

"Do you know what I mean?" her friend is asking her, without really asking the way she does.

The mother is on the phone with her friend. What were they talking about? "Mm-hmm," the mother says. "Right."

"It's like, I can't do everything all the time for everyone, right?" The friend laughs. "I mean, who can?"

"Right," the mother says.

"No one, that's who."

"Right," the mother says. "And you shouldn't have to. Because no one can."

"That's right," the friend says. "That's exactly right. Thank you."

"For what?"

The friend says, "For being such a good listener."

———

SOMETIMES THE mother lets the children stay alone in the house with Marcus, although the girl protests, says she doesn't want to be babysat by Marcus, no way, you've got to be kidding me. Please say you are kidding me, because this isn't funny. Marcus, our baby-sitter? On which planet does that make sense, Mars or Jupiter? Maybe Neptune? Because on Earth—you've heard of Earth, right? The one with that whole green-and-blue marbly thing going on?—leaving us with Marcus as our babysitter makes about as much sense as leaving us with no one at all, which, by the way, seems about ten thousand times better an idea to me than leaving us with Marcus. Now that I think about it, why don't we just go with that plan? You and Cliff can take Marcus with you? Hey, that's a great idea! Just picture it, the three of you sitting together at a bar, Marcus sucking down his third Roy Rogers. Who's the kid? People will love that.

"He's not babysitting you," the mother sighs. "He's just watching over things for a very short period of time."

"Define short," the girl says.

"Short means short," the mother says.

"Whatever," the girl says.

"Short means I'm your mother and I'm telling you we won't be gone long."

The girl says, "I liked your first try better."

But Marcus isn't a terrible babysitter, even if the girl won't admit it. For the most part, he leaves her alone and keeps out of sight, two qualities she values in a caregiver. It's not like those nights when the babysitter watches them, blaring his music and polishing off the last of the ice cream — the children have witnessed the babysitter inhale a pint of cherry vanilla straight from the carton — or talking nonstop about his car. With Marcus in charge, the girl can exercise a little bit of freedom, so the girl exercises a little bit of freedom. She closes the door to her room and reads all the celebrity magazines her mother steals from work. The girl feels superior to and jealous of these actors and actresses and models and musicians, this beautiful tribe of troubled people whose insights into the world are so dull, banal, and insipid ("I consider myself to be a very spiritual person, but then again, I can be, like, totally in your face too") that it takes everything the girl has to make it to the end of an interview. She's better off sticking to the ads, where, mercifully, the beautiful people have not been tasked with anything greater than tossing their too-shiny hair across their enviable shoulders. The girl turns slick page after slick page. Her fingers exude the smell of perfume.

Downstairs, Marcus and the boy tour the basement, looking for things to light on fire. Marcus has a lighting-on-fire system that's both practical and clever: first, you find something you don't want anymore, some old toy, say, or something that doesn't belong to you at all but is likely of low interest to anyone, holiday items, for example, or family heirlooms, and then you carry it to the back deck, where the object of no affection can be safely torched on the grill. Master techniques: close grill lid to deter attention-calling smoke. Douse smoldering object with multitude-of-sins-covering hose water, wrap torched/unloved object in newspaper and discard newspaper-wrapped object in kitchen garbage bag balled with other decoy newspaper wads, so as to discourage prominence of wet, bulging newspaper wad, pregnant with immolated Santa Claus figurine. Hide lighter for future use.

Half the business of being a boy, the girl thinks, watching her brother and Marcus from her bedroom window, is to answer the question, *What's the most inane thing I could possibly be doing right now?* Marcus is instructing her brother to hold the grill lid while Marcus sparks a lighter to a plush toy's ear. Her brother is hopping in place, the way he does when he's excited, the dumb slob. Probably needed to go to the bathroom twenty minutes ago. Marcus urges her brother to step away, then squirts lighter fluid on the toy, a stupid gorilla her brother used to carry around with him when he was a toddler. Goo-Goo the gorilla. His favorite, back then. Her brother is probably too scared to say anything to Marcus. Afraid Marcus will call him a baby, which he absolutely would, and which would be a mean thing to say, no matter how accurate. Stand up to him, the girl thinks. Grab that gorilla! Save Goo-Goo! But her brother only hops up and down like a maniac. Goo-Goo smolders and burns, his smiling head aflame.

And it occurs to the girl that her brother is hopping in part because he wants to rescue poor Goo-Goo but can't bring himself to do it.

————

THE LINES: Cars stretch for blocks outside the gas station. People start lining up at five o'clock in the morning, some even earlier, the boy has seen it on the news. The cars are still there when the boy's mother drives the children to the store, to the supermarket, to the bank, where the children are still young enough to receive a Dum-Dum lollipop from the teller, the lollipop still bulging from their sugary mouths when they pass the station again. The intersection, choked with cars, seems a malevolent place.

The entrance sign reads: WE HAVE GAS BUT GOVENOR

DUPONT SAYS WE MUST RATION IF YOU DON'T LIKE IT LET HIM KNOW.

———

ONE NIGHT, the girl is standing in front of the bathroom mirror, deciding whether she looks older from the left side or the right, when she hears the telephone ring. Her mother and Cliff are both working late again, and her brother and Marcus are off doing whatever, the girl couldn't care less really, but whatever it is, it's keeping them from answering the phone by the fourth ring, so the girl races to her mother's room, dives across the bed, and snags the phone receiver all in one motion. "Hello?" she says, a little out of breath.

"Well, the rumors you've heard are true," Gumma says. "I'm trapped in a hurricane."

"Oh," the girl says, but Gumma is already describing the boards she had to put up by herself across her windows.

"You think they would make them so it could be a one-person job, but oh no, they've got to make them so you can barely hold them in place without leaning one side against a ladder. Took me fifteen minutes and one broken kitchen chair to figure that one out, and do you think I'm ever going to see the money for that chair? No way, Jose. I've got about the same chance of getting that money as I've got that someone will help me take down all these boards when the storm is over, which is pretty much zilch."

The girl can hear the familiar slosh and clink of margarita ice, a sound she didn't realize she was nostalgic for until now.

"It's like I always told your mother about putting up a Christmas tree by myself. I said, 'Why would I put up a Christmas tree for nobody? Why would I go through all that trouble when no one is going to see it besides me?' And she would say 'Oh, the holidays this, and Oh, the holidays that,' and then I would say, 'You know no one is going to help me take it down when the holidays are over? You know that, don't you?' and then she would say, 'Oh, I would help you take it down if I could,' but what else was she going to say? I knew if I put up a tree, I'd have to do it all by myself, and then sure as hell I'd be the one to take it down all by myself. You can't count on anyone anymore. All you can count on is yourself."

The girl hears a sudden thunderclap in the background, a forceful booming that lasts the length of a dotted whole note and makes it impossible to determine how Gumma has transitioned from the subject of Christmas trees to bank tellers.

"Oh, they've got this one teller at my bank I don't like. I don't like her one bit. Shifty, you know? Like she can't even look you in the eye? If I'm standing in line and I see she's going to be my teller, I let the next person go ahead of me. And I know she sees me do it. She knows I don't trust her. Because she's after my money. That's why I don't trust her. I say to the person in line, You go right ahead of me, that's right. I don't want that shifty-eyed teller."

Another thunderclap. "Gumma?" the girl says. "Are you OK?"

But Gumma only spends the next five minutes talking about her financial advisor, Mr. Not-So-Bright, who still hasn't called her back like he promised, and who is probably in cahoots with that shifty bank teller, Gumma wouldn't be surprised. Of all the things that wouldn't surprise her in the least, Mr. Not-So-Bright being in cahoots with that shifty bank teller would be at the top of the list, that's for sure. The two of them probably think it's a riot, stealing her money together.

"Gumma?" the girl says, but there's only more thunder, and then the line goes dead.

———

A FEW NIGHTS after the father's imagined conversation with Sarah, he parks his car at the far end of the restaurant parking

lot and tries to spot her with his son's binoculars, a serious challenge for a variety of reasons. One: the father isn't sure if Sarah is
even working tonight. Two: the parking lot lights are brighter than
he expected and make him feel exposed, foolish. Three: the binoculars are for children; he can't adjust them to his adult-spaced
eyes without the binoculars threatening to break and so must hold
them a few inches from his face, which either makes the restaurant windows appear much closer or much farther away, he can't
quite tell. Four: his breath keeps fogging up the car's windows, but
he doesn't want to crack them open, even a little, for fear of mos-
quitoes. The father spends the next twenty minutes in this manner, the windows acquiring additional coats of exhalation, the binoculars simultaneously drawing the restaurant near and urging it
away. Should the father turn on the air conditioner? Or will that
give him away? A compromise: the father opens the windows but
gives up on the binoculars. There. Better. And the father is just
feeling brave enough to try the binoculars again when it starts to
rain.

———

MARCUS CAN'T believe the children have to go to church, even
though the children have explained that they really don't go anymore, not often, anyway.

"Whatever," Marcus says. "I wouldn't go to that church for all
the money in the world."

The girl says, "We don't get paid to go to church."

The boy says, "You give them the money? In the basket?"

Marcus laughs. "Oh, you give them your money, all right, that's
for sure. Then they give it all to the pope."

The girl says that's stupid; the money doesn't go to the pope.
The money goes to the church and to the parish. And to the poor.
Their church even sponsors a food kitchen in the inner city. The

girl tells Marcus about the time she volunteered there for a school project, how she got to serve cranberry sauce as part of a free Thanksgiving meal.

"It wasn't free," Marcus says, then raises his index finger, as if to instruct. "No such thing as a free meal."

The girl says it was free. "I was there," she reminds him.

"There's no such thing as a free meal," Marcus intones. "Plus, the pope is the Antichrist."

"What's the Antichrist?" the boy says.

"Read your Bible sometime," Marcus says. "You'll see."

The girl sighs. "The pope is not the Antichrist. That's stupid."

Marcus shrugs. "Suit yourself," he says, "but that's what my mom always said. Catholic Church, biggest cult in the world." Marcus clicks his tongue. "She always said the Catholic Church was the whores of Babylon."

"What's that?" the boy says.

"He doesn't even know," the girl says. "He's just trying to show off again."

"The whores of Babylon," Marcus repeats. "Doesn't sound too good, does it?"

"But what is it?" the boy asks.

"It's your church," Marcus says. "That's what."

"Don't listen to him," the girl says. "He has no idea what he's talking about."

"Don't call anybody your father," Marcus says. "That's in there too. Look it up."

"What about calling your father your father?" the boy asks. "You mean you're not supposed to?" At times like these, the girl wants to crumple her brother up into a ball and toss him into a wastebasket. She does. The way he gives in to Marcus's stupid ideas, again and again, no matter how ridiculous they are. The girl isn't sure which is in greater supply, Marcus's stupid ideas or her brother's interest in them. Either way, this chewing gum has lost its flavor. How many more weeks until school begins?

"You call your daddy your daddy," Marcus says.

"What about 'dad'?" the boy says.

"There's nothing against that," Marcus admits.

"I usually just say 'dad,'" the boy says. "Unless it's Father's Day."

"Father's Day was invented by Hallmark," Marcus says.

———

SINCE CLIFF moved in, things that never worked suddenly work. The dining room light dimmer dims. The kitchen blinds lower and raise without tangling. The garbage disposal the children had always been warned not to use — see this switch here? Don't touch it, ever! — dismisses broccoli stalks with the same indifference it turns on pizza crusts and granola. Someone has oiled the hinges on all the upstairs closet doors so that they no longer creak or sigh. Flashlights that haven't had batteries since forever now work so that the girl can check inside the dryer for coins. She's been making a little money on laundry detail, not much, but some. The dryer's interior, illuminated, seems a disappointing cave sheltering hibernating towels and warm nickels. Someone has arranged all the worthless items in the kitchen junk drawer into like kinds. How did the family acquire so many pencils?

As much as Cliff rearranges and repairs things, he will not touch the kitchen table. There, the mother's stacks of letters, bills, catalogs, textbooks, notebooks, and index cards stand next to canned goods yet to be put away, boxes of pasta, jars of grape jelly. One day, when no one is around, the girl tries something: she takes a handful of pencils from the junk drawer and places them in various places around the kitchen table. She puts a pencil beneath a textbook, tucks another inside a notebook, and leaves others sandwiched between piles, only their chewed erasers sticking out. The pencils remain where the girl leaves them for days, then a week, then more. The girl is disappointed. Cliff has failed her test; even his fastidiousness has its limits. The house has drifted off course, and there isn't much Cliff can do about it really. To let him off the hook, the girl decides to remove the pencils from their hiding spots, intending to put them away. And that's when she discovers that someone has sharpened each one into a perfect point.

––––––––

ONE AFTERNOON, the mother tells the boy she has an idea. She would like him and Marcus to collect as many cans as they can find in the neighborhood, and she will pay them five cents for each can. How does that sound? To help them on the road to financial and environmental success, she will spot them fifty cents each in the unlikely event that they are unable to find any cans; she will also supply them with garbage bags and work gloves, if they would like to wear work gloves, that is.

"I don't want to wear gloves," the boy says.

"I understand," the mother says.

"Marcus won't either."

"OK," the mother says, nods. "That's what I figured."

The boy doesn't understand why the mother wants him and Marcus to find cans and knows his next question should be "Why do you want us to find cans?" but sometimes his questions do a funny thing where they duck and hide and send out a surrogate question in their place, so what comes out now is "Where will we find cans?"

The mother says he'll be surprised by how many they'll find; people litter everywhere. Tells him she knows they'll find some cans near the neighborhood entrance, a great place to start, she's sure of it.

"OK," the boy says, although he feels like he's missing something, he doesn't know quite what. But it will be nice to make money, right? his thoughts supply, steering him elsewhere, the way they sometimes do. He can even put the money in the coin bank. If he wants to.

The boy would like to ask Marcus what's going on, but even Marcus seems distracted, a rarity for him; you can always sort of count on Marcus to be Marcus, something the boy didn't realize he relied on really until now. He and Marcus walk to the neighborhood entrance, their fingers clutching garbage bags, empty, embarrassing. The boy keeps expecting Marcus to say how collecting cans is a waste of time—Marcus has already explained how recycling is a Russian ploy to make us live in our own garbage—but Marcus doesn't say anything, not even when the two of them reach the entrance and idly search for cans in the weedy undergrowth across the way, no cars this time of day, their task boring, pointless, a grind. Marcus finds three cans to the boy's one, a crushed Lipton's choked with dirt, but doesn't even brag about it or make fun of the boy when he daintily shakes the dirt from the Lipton's can before tossing it into his bag. After a while, Marcus says he's going to take a break, this heat is a bitch. The boy says he's going to keep looking for a little while longer, but Marcus tells him to come sit with him on this rock for a while, there's space for him too. Which is strange. The boy sits next to Marcus, who twists a long spear of grass into rope.

"I'm going to tell you some things, OK?" Marcus says.

"OK," the boy says.

"But after I tell you, I don't want you asking me questions about it, got it?"

"OK."

"Not one goddamned question."

"I won't," the boy says. "I promise."

"OK," Marcus says, then exhales, somewhat dramatically. "Here

goes." And what Marcus tells the boy next, about what happens between a man and a woman in the bedroom late at night, when they
are naked and want to be naked, when they decide to do something specific with their naked bodies, and how that something
leads to babies being born, including the boy, including himself,
including everyone, is so precisely detailed with so many impossible happenings, things the boy had no idea about whatsoever,
that the only way the boy could begin to grasp what Marcus is saying would be to ask question after question, which he has promised not to do, and which would betray his lack of knowledge about
men and women and babies, that it is all the boy can do to summon an expression that suggests he already knows what Marcus
is telling him, this is all nothing new, he's aware of these secrets,
bored even. But this thing is happening where his legs won't stop
bouncing up and down, even as he says "Uh-huh" to every notion-
exploding word from Marcus's lips.

"But," the boy says.

"No questions."

"I wasn't," the boy protests.

"You were," Marcus says.

And a funny thing happens later, after they return home and
the boy's mother asks him how many cans he found, when the
boy momentarily understands that his mother put Marcus up to
telling him about the men and women and babies and likely paid
him for it too. Yes, the boy thinks, that's what happened. And right
behind that thought is another, wherein he understands that his
mother was too afraid to talk to him herself, yet too hesitant to
ask Cliff to do it — Cliff, who probably would have done a better
job, kind Cliff, patient Cliff — but ended up handing the task to
Marcus, and then greasing Marcus's reluctant gears with a little
cash. Yes, that's all so clear to the boy now; it's like he's looking
across a great distance as one unrecognizable shape becomes a

recognizable one, over and over again, an alarming rate of clarity that's new and unprecedented. This must be what growing up will be like, yes. Maybe the rest of his life will be like this from now on, a clear view of everything everyone else already understands, wherein the boy embraces complexity, contradiction, and possibility—a notion that's either thrilling or terrifying or both. Which one? The boy feels he's on the verge of revelation, but then he pulls the dirty Lipton's can from the bag and his mind is on to the next thing, which is that he never wants to collect cans again.

———

ONE NIGHT, on her drive home from work, the mother sees a dead cat on the side of the road, the same size and color as the family cat. No, she thinks, please God, no. Their cat couldn't possibly have wandered this far from home—the mother is two miles away, two and a half even—could he? Not their cat. No way. Not a chance. Their cat is more of a linger-in-the-neighborhood-type cat, not a highway traveler. Sure, he disappears from time to time, but can't they always count on him to show up at the kitchen door, looking for food, company? No wanderlust for their cat. Set him out on the open highway, and he'd only nap safely in the shade. Dream of gelatinous food scooped from stinky tins. Sleep. Wake. Wander home, bored.

But it is their cat. No mistaking that fur, that tail. Those white paws. No. This is their wandering cat after all, come home to die. No. The mother pulls her car to the side of the road, tries to figure out what to do. At this time of night, cars pass only occasionally, slowing to pass the mother, whose car idles with its hazard signals on, as the mother cries quietly into a McDonald's napkin and imagines how she will break the news to the children. The night is close and humid, reluctant to guide the mother's thoughts, which keep making turns into blind alley after blind alley. Dim stars, barely visible through dense trees, withhold consolation. We have no idea either, they seem to say. When the mother's imagination informs her that she will not, in fact, be able to break the news to the children, she gets a different idea altogether: she will bury the cat and, in a way, protect the children from knowing. They will never see the cat's lifeless body, lying here, with its legs in strange and incorrect repose. She will keep the cat's death a secret. That's something she can do for the children. Yes.

But when she dares to leave her car and approach the cat, the sight of the cat's mouth, open just so, and revealing a dark rim of blood around the cat's dark gums, brings different news altogether: she will not be able to bury the cat. Not a chance. Why is it that life, which the mother has always credited as having a keen sense of humor, has only recently begun to show its mean streak, sending up one more challenge several leagues beyond the mother's skill set? The wind picks up, as if to mock. Cars, passing, neglect to switch to low beams, bathing the mother in too-bright light. The mother, glimpsed in passing: a woman in her early thirties, windblown hair, unremarkable dress, sobbing into a napkin. In the rearview mirror: a small woman diminishing into an even smaller woman diminishing into nothing at all. This mother is out of her depth. She needs someone else to bury this animal, someone to protect her children from the sight of the dead cat, and when that person is so obvious and readily available and so certain to say yes, it is all the mother can do to burst into grateful tears when, a few minutes later, after the mother has pulled into the gas station and inserted a dime into the payphone, she hears Cliff say he will take care of it, of course.

FOURTEEN

TWO WEEKS before school starts, on another idiotic night when Marcus is supposedly watching the children, the girl slips out of the house. Whoosh! Gone. She has a plan, the girl does, but it is only half-formed at best; the other half she'll improvise, she figures, make it up on the fly. Plan: ask the babysitter to drive her to Sarah's house. Other half of plan: but where exactly does Sarah live, and why would the babysitter drive her there, and what would the girl say is the reason in the first place, and is the babysitter even home? Is Sarah home? The girl considers these questions, weighs options. Her neighborhood is quiet this time of night, save for the occasional barking dog or passing car — the girl lowers her head, looks away. These streets, the source of so much childhood consolation, have accepted the girl's Halloween trick or treating as readily as they've endured her roller skating, and in winter, when hidden beneath a veil of snow, have held the shape of her footprints until long after she's returned home and removed her boots. It is not dark yet, but already she must seem out of place, this girl out on a solo stroll, sporting jean shorts and a halter top she's been experimenting with feeling OK about wearing in public. Will Sarah approve?

The girl presses the babysitter's doorbell, but the doorbell doesn't work. Knocks. Rehearses what she will say when the babysitter opens the door, when the babysitter opens the door and says, "Am I supposed to be babysitting you tonight?" His look is one of true confusion, amplified by his lack of shirt, shoes, socks, and possibly shower. His hair sticks up straight, like he's just woken up for the day.

"Who is it?" a voice says, and the babysitter's friend materializes beside him. Her expression is dazed.

"It's one of the kids I babysit," the babysitter says. "With that bank?"

"Were you supposed to babysit them tonight?" the friend asks.

"That's what I asked her," the babysitter says.

"Was he?" the friend asks.

The girl says no, then explains: her dad asked her to get a ride to his girlfriend's house — this is the first time the girl has used that word to describe Sarah, how sad to think it probably no longer applies — but her mom is working tonight. It's kind of important that she get a ride. She's super-sorry to have to ask, and she knows the answer is probably no, but could he maybe drive her there? She's so sorry to bug them with this, she really is. She could even pay them when they get there.

"This girl is on a journey of epic proportions," the babysitter's friend says slowly, then laughs a strange laugh; the two of them have been drinking or worse, the girl realizes.

The babysitter waves a dismissive hand. "Your money isn't any good to us," he says.

"That doesn't make sense," the friend says.

"It means, like," the babysitter says, "even though your money would be good to us, we're going to pretend like we don't want it."

The two of them laugh. Kiss. They tell the girl to wait outside, they'll drive her, sure, why not. "Let the journey begin," the friend says.

Five minutes later, they are in the babysitter's Pontiac, the babysitter behind the wheel, the friend in the passenger's seat, and the girl in the back. The windows are down, the radio on, loud. How strange it feels to ride in the back of this car, where the girl must share the seat with a guitar case and an amplifier, a seat belt across its bulbous front. The babysitter says he's no good with directions, but if the girl can just give him lefts and rights, he should do just fine. The girl asks him if he knows how to get to that gas station at the intersection? The one with the sign? If he can get to the gas station with the sign, she should be able to figure it out from there.

"That gas station is crazy!" the babysitter says, then mentions he had to wait in line for an hour and half this morning and still didn't get any gas. "But that sign, man. Kills me."

"So wait," the friend says, "you did or didn't get gas?"

"Didn't," the babysitter says. "Couldn't."

"So," the friend says, then leans her head so she can read the dashboard. "We're going to run out of gas?"

"Nah," the babysitter says. His driving style, the girl observes, in comparison to her father's, is heavy on wandering close the shoulder, then drifting back into the lane. Also, crossing the center line, every now and then. "Probably not. Maybe."

They approach the gas station, that familiar intersection, but even from a distance the girl can tell something is off tonight. The gas station's massive roof—the one that shelters twin islands with four pumps apiece and the little convenience mart the girl has known since forever—is brightly lit, like always, all signs of life, commerce, and enterprise; but beneath the roof, the pumps are dark, the islands empty. No cars. No trucks. No one topping off their pricey purchase with a squeeze of a slick nozzle. Instead, a line of cars and trucks haphazardly blocks one of the station's entrances, while a flatbed trailer, purposely turned it seems, blocks the station's only other entrance. A small crowd stands on the sidewalk, idly smoking and talking with one another, and it isn't until the babysitter pulls up close that the girl realizes these people must be the drivers of the cars blocking the entranceways. From this distance, the girl can read the gas station sign: JUMPIN' JACK FLASH IS A GAS BUT WE'RE OUT SORRY.

"Oh man," the babysitter says. "That sucks."

The babysitter's friend says their journey has taken a dark turn, then lights a cigarette with the car's lighter, a thrilling, fiery knob the girl has never seen anyone actually use before.

"What are all these people doing out here?" the babysitter says.

"Waiting for whatever," the friend says. "What else?" She exhales, puts her feet up on the dash. The babysitter says not to put her feet on the dash, on the account of how he's trying to keep the car clean?

The friend ignores him, asks the girl, "So where are we going again?"

"Take a left at the next light," the girl says. But she wants to know what all those people are doing too. She can see them out the back window, inscrutable in the station's glow. If she could just take a longer look, everything would reveal itself to her, the way it sometimes does. The babysitter takes a left at the next light and the station disappears from view, and it's like the world keeps adding one mystery after another.

———

IT'S NOT THAT the boy can't stand up for himself really, it's more that he doesn't want Marcus to feel unwelcome in their house is all. Especially with the summer winding down and Marcus about to return to Texas, to where his mom lives. Plus, Marcus's school starts a week earlier than the children's school. Unfair. Soon, he'll have to pack up his things and bid the children adieu, even though the children will still have one week of summer left to waste, which is sad when you think about it. So what's wrong with letting Marcus douse the Smash Up Derby cars with a little lighter fluid and torching them on the grill? Nothing, that's what, the boy's teary eyes notwithstanding. Too much smoke is the problem there. See it rising from the derby car's wheels, an oily ribbon turning in the breeze? Tear-maker, that smoke. And it's not like Marcus has any idea what the derby cars are or what they mean to the boy or how angry the girl would be if she knew the two of them were out on the deck roasting them like marshmallows. She isn't even around, seems like, which makes it doubly OK to assist Marcus by slightly lowering the grill lid so that the second derby car can catch fire without another pesky breeze having its way. It's fine if the boy agrees that the cars look cool on fire, like they've just been in a wreck, since agreeing is the nice thing to do, and since agreeing diverts Marcus's attention from the tears gathering in the boy's eyes. Polite masterstroke: wipe eyes on the sly, while Marcus is busy administering another squirt of fluid, so as to not distract him from his task. In a way, the boy's politeness is superior to standing up for himself. This way no one gets angry or upset. Always a good thing.

"Too damn windy," Marcus says.

"Yeah," the boy says, tasting tears.

"What's up with your face?" Marcus asks, regarding him.

"Nothing," the boy says. "Smoke."

"You should see your face. It looks all horrible."

The boy turns away and inhales a giant, tear-reversing breath, before wiping his eyes again. "The smoke," he says. "I think I'm allergic?"

Marcus laughs his cheerless laugh. "You can't be allergic to *smoke*," he says. "That's the stupidest thing I've ever heard in my life." He holds the lighter to the drenched derby car. The car bursts into flames. "Medically impossible."

Beyond the deck, the boy's neighborhood administers a heavy dose of nature, so many trees and hills and grasses and weeds and streams, it's dizzying to think of it all, no end to it really. Backyards seem to face nature, the boy realizes, an invitation to the wild, while front yards seem to face the other way, toward all the roads leading elsewhere, toward highways and towns and cities. Houses are trapped between two worlds then, a little bit on the side of nature and a little bit against nature too. This, a thought the boy might share with Marcus if Marcus wasn't so busy trying to coax the Smash Up Derby cars into flames.

———

THE MOTHER and Cliff are meeting up with some of the mother's work friends for a few drinks. Always a risky proposition, mixing Cliff and work. There's a part of her life the mother wants to keep private, but lately she's gotten Cliff's not-terribly-hard-to-read signals that he wants to be included in events like this and her friends invited her out anyway and Cliff will be moving out soon and the mother wants to forestall another private conversation about the future of their relationship, so the mother compromised, and compromise has led them here, to a restaurant bar where Cliff nods politely as the mother's coworkers gossip about people Cliff has never met and will never meet. Maybe that's why Cliff seems comfortable laughing along with them, nothing to lose, kind Cliff. Poor Cliff. Not much of a drinker, but he buys the second round anyway. The mother stirs her gin and tonic in a desultory way. Is Cliff as apprehensive about the ride home as she is, or is she only nervous because she knows something Cliff does not know—namely, that she's going to tell him they should consider taking a break for a while? She needs some time to sort of clear her head. With summer ending and the children going back to school. And the separation yielding to divorce, as it certainly will. That's going to be a lot to deal with, and he shouldn't feel obligated to shoulder any of that load. In a way, she feels like she's using him as a means of putting off the inevitable. In a way. And she doesn't want to be that person, you know? She couldn't live with herself if she were that person. So she hopes he understands why she needs a little time to herself, for herself, but also for her family. God, she feels so cheap dragging her family into it, but there it is.

She can already imagine Cliff nodding that maddening and agreeable nod of his. Imagine him agreeing to whatever she says. Even if what she wants is for him to say, "I'm not going anywhere."

Is that what she wants?

"Maybe," the mother says, then realizes she's talking out loud again.

———

WHAT THE babysitter's friend wants to know is, does the girl love herself? Does she? She should think about it before she answers. Don't just say yes because you think that's what you're supposed to say. Tell the truth. Reason for asking is, you have to love yourself before someone can love you back, it's true. The girl says she doesn't know, she guesses she does, but how would she be able to tell?

"Oh, you'd know," the friend explains. She exhales a plume of smoke out the passenger window. "It's like, do you know that song, 'Feelings'?"

The girl says she doesn't know that song.

"Well, that's what it's like," the friend says, "it's like that song."

The babysitter says that song is lame, turns up the radio, some rock song the girl doesn't know. For the past few minutes, the babysitter's friend has been asking the girl about her parent's separation, what happened, how she feels about it, what it's like for her dad to have a new girlfriend. At first the girl felt threatened, invaded, but soon discovered that there's a freedom in talking to a stranger about your life, especially a stranger like the babysitter's friend, who nods at everything the girl says, like she knew the girl was going to say that before she said it, and has this way of closing her eyes after she speaks that makes it look like she's either lost in contemplation or about to fall asleep. Talking to the friend is like talking to no one and everyone all at once. So the girl talks.

"Here," the friend says, turns to the girl, and hands her a ring. "Try this on."

The girl has one of these at home, everyone does, but plays along like the ring is a novelty, says, "How pretty."

The friend explains that the ring will tell them the girl's mood. "Hold it up so I can see."

The girl complies. "It's black. What does black mean?"

The friend takes the ring back. "It's always black," she says. "I think it's broken."

"Bummer," the babysitter says.

Later, the friend tells the girl she needs to forgive her father; the girl should trust her, she knows from experience. The friend closes her eyes, exhales another cloud of cigarette smoke. Says she spent years hating her father, and all that hate was like a giant, sour ball inside her, growing and growing until it couldn't grow anymore. Ran out of space. So, what happened? She finally decided to find the courage to forgive her father. Just like that. And you know what? It was the best decision she ever made in her life. "Took a lot of bravery," the friend says, "a whole lot."

The girl, who doesn't recall saying anything that would suggest she hates her father and who doesn't feel like she hates her father really, not at any level that would require forgiveness, Sarah's departure notwithstanding, says, "You were brave."

———

BUT WHAT could possess Marcus to do what he does next, which is look up from the disappointing remains of the Smash Up Derby cars and say, "Hey, what about that stupid bank?" He prods the cars with a grilling fork. The cars have melted in unappealing ways and give off a burning smell that seems trapped inside the boy's nose; he might never get it out.

"The bank?" the boy says.

"Yeah," Marcus says. "That stupid bank of yours."

"But," the boy says, "it's metal?"

"So? Metal melts."

"Well," the boy says.

"We could melt it down and split the money," Marcus says. "Fifty-fifty." For the first time today that the boy can recall, Marcus smiles.

"Well," the boy says.

But Marcus is already heading past him, through the sliding glass doors and into the house. The boy follows, his stomach doing this weird somersault-thing he didn't know it could do. He trails Marcus up the stairs to his bedroom. There, Marcus scoops the bank from the boy's desk and holds it to the light, inspecting it. "Too thick to melt," he says, "but the door might melt, just a little." He presses the door with his blackened fingers. "Enough to get the money out."

The boy reminds him that it's not much money. He even said so. Remember?

Marcus shrugs. "Beats nothing."

And Marcus is about to push past the boy, the bank in hand, when the boy discovers he's said something to Marcus he's never said to Marcus before, a word as familiar and alien to the boy as his mother's first name.

"No," he says.

Marcus laughs. "No?"

The boy makes another discovery: he's positioned himself in the doorway with his arms outstretched, hands braced against the doorjamb. "No."

"You've got to be kidding me," Marcus says.

"Put the bank down," the boy says.

Marcus laughs his infrequent laugh, the one he reserves for TV shows that aren't funny, plus ugly pets. "Put the bank down, ha," he says. "You should see yourself."

"Put it down," the boy says.

"Move," Marcus says, grabbing the boy's trembling shoulder.

The boy braces himself in the doorway, his hands gripping the jamb. They should make special handrails for occasions like these, the boy thinks. This, the boy's last thought before Marcus pushes him to the floor.

———

HE SHOULD just call Sarah, the father should. It wouldn't be a big deal if he did. Even if he said he wouldn't. Because solitude has given him a chance to put some things in perspective and has helped him see how it doesn't really matter whether he calls Sarah just like she said he would. Because there's no value in avoiding doing something you want to do just because you said you wouldn't. That's arrogance, plain and simple, the father's loneliness would have him know. That's all it really is. That, plus vanity. Plus pride. And the thing is, if you let arrogance, vanity and pride rule your life, what kind of person are you? Not a fully actualized one, that's for sure, or at least not a sentient one. Because the father picking up the telephone right now and dialing Sarah's number might be a blow to his pride, but it would also be an affirmation of his self-worth and humility too. That's the thing about the father, he can be humble, even if he's the last person who would ever point that out. Not his style. And the thing about Sarah is that she would recognize his humility, his total refusal of vanity and arrogance, and understand that his solitude had led him, not without some first-class soul-searching, to this moment. That's something Sarah would totally grasp. The father feels he can count on that from Sarah at least. Her mood would be conciliatory, open. Possibly enthusiastic. Thankful, even.

He should just call Sarah.

———

THE ONE TIME the girl accompanied Sarah to her neighborhood, Sarah had needed to run inside to grab her bathing suit; the girl waited in the car with her brother while Sarah dashed inside and returned a few moments later, pool bag in hand, ready to go. Just a glimpse of Sarah's driveway, garage, and front porch, but enough that now, driving through Sarah's neighborhood as night falls, the girl feels she can find Sarah's house again if she takes a good, long look at each one. But she cannot do that tonight, no, not with the babysitter's car about to run out of gas, and the babysitter's friend advising her that if you love something, you must let it go. If it comes back, it is yours; if not, it was never meant to be.

"It might be this one," the girl says as they slow in front of yet another house, this one nearly identical to the last. A squat rancher with two rocking chairs on the porch, geraniums hanging from plastic pots. "No, sorry."

"That's OK," the babysitter says, but even the girl can see, from the back seat, the wan glow of the low fuel signal, a hieroglyphed gas pump the color of a halved mango. The babysitter's friend says she doesn't want to be a downer, but they're going to need some gas soon, so maybe they could come back later? Like after they find some gas? Maybe they could even call the father's girlfriend, you know, to let her know what's up? The friend says she'd be glad to call, if the girl wants her to.

And that's when the girl finds herself saying, "It's that one, right there." A little lie that feels necessary, warranted. The girl says, "That's her car in the driveway," and, as a masterstroke, "I just saw her in the window," as the babysitter slows to the curb and then pulls away at the girl's insistence, who says she doesn't want them to risk another minute. Don't run out of gas. Go on. She doesn't want to hold them up.

So why is the girl disappointed when they pull away without even making sure that she got inside safely? The girl waves good-bye from this stranger's front porch, praying that no one will hear her and open the door. When the babysitter's Pontiac disappears from view, the girl hops down from the porch and begins a tour of Sarah's neighborhood. So many houses. So many front lawns, so many driveways. The neighborhood, indifferent to the girl's objective, offers up one more indistinguishable home after another, while the sky makes up its mind about a full moon. Maybe, maybe not. Maybe later.

———

MARCUS HAS turned many expressions on the boy over the past few months, but he must have kept this one hidden, because the boy has never seen this one before, a sort of amused bewilderment undercut with something unprecedented and hard to read, and it isn't until Marcus looks up from the grill, where he has just doused the bank with lighter fluid, that the boy reads it, clearly, unmistakably: fear.

"What are you supposed to be?" Marcus laughs. "A majorette?"

The boy is holding the girl's marching baton. He raises it before him and motions toward the grill. "Take the bank off of there," he says.

"Or what? You'll twirl me?" Marcus laughs, but his laugh has been robbed of its usual menace, swapped out with uncertainty. Challenge Marcus and you'll find another, much smaller Marcus lurking behind him. This baton is wanting the boy to know so much. The boy is willing to follow it around for a while and see where it leads. Marcus produces a lighter from wherever, summons a breezed flame.

The boy steps closer. "Don't make me," he says. He's close enough to strike Marcus, he is.

Marcus holds the flame to the bank. "Here comes the twirler," Marcus says. "Strike up the band."

The boy can see Marcus now, the real Marcus. The real Marcus is just some kid, like him, not much older, not enough to matter, anyway. Bigger, sure, but not much. Has no idea about half the things he talks about. Talks just to convince himself of what he's saying. The boy sees Marcus's eyes dart to the baton, to the boy, and back again. Should have picked up this baton years ago. "Now," the boy says, his voice surprising and strange.

"OK," Marcus says. "But first give us a twirl."

And that's when Marcus grabs the baton. The two of them stand for a moment, two boys clutching a girl's marching baton in front of a grill on which a coin bank glitteringly burns, slick with lighter fluid, thick smoke curling into the air. The boy pulls against Marcus's grip, but it's no use. Marcus drags the boy to his knees in an instant, the boy still clinging to the baton, his fingers burning with effort. He can feel the baton slipping away. A few more seconds of this and it will be over. His fingers reach the end of the baton, cling to the rubber stopper. He's about to let go of the stopper when Marcus tumbles backward and falls hard onto the deck, the other rubber stopper in his hand. The secret stopper. The one that opens. A half dozen slips of paper spill from the baton, like dead butterflies. The wind takes them, deposits them atop the deck, at the base of the grill, against the picnic table, whose umbrella quakes in the breeze. One disappears off the side of the deck. Another lands at the boy's knees, close enough that he can read his sister's careful handwriting—*Don't be a stealer!!*—before it too blows away to wherever. The boy rises to his feet, holds the baton in a defensive pose. He's not at all ready for what's next, but armed against what's next nonetheless. Marcus says he's going to kick the boy's ass, stands from the deck and grabs the baton again. Something tells the boy to let the baton go, so he lets the baton go.

"That was easy," Marcus says, then does something the boy does not expect: he hits him with the baton, right across his arm. This hurts. This hurts a lot. The boy has rarely felt this kind of pain. The boy screams.

Marcus says, "Sorry, but you made me do that, right?"

It's like his arm is on fire, the boy would say, if anyone asked him, which they haven't. He cries and cries.

"OK, stop it," Marcus says. "Please? OK? Stop it, or you're going to wake up the whole goddamn neighborhood."

But the boy cannot stop it.

"Well, you shouldn't have made me hit you then," Marcus says. "Plus, I said sorry. So that's it. So shut up."

"They don't use *embalming fluid* on *pretzels!*" the boy cries.

"Aw, you're just mad at me now," Marcus says.

"And garbage men aren't *millionaires!*"

"Well," Marcus says, "some of them are."

"None of them!" the boy cries. The pain surges in his arm. "Not one!" He's got this horrible snot rope hanging from his nostril, but he doesn't even bother to wipe it away. "That's why they're *garbage men.* If they were millionaires, they wouldn't be garbage men. Everybody knows that."

"Listen," Marcus says, "you're getting yourself all worked up because I hit you. But I said sorry, so why don't you run inside and have yourself a nice little cry and we'll just say everything is even, OK?"

"You have no common sense!" the boy says.

"OK, big man, I hear you."

"You're just a stupid kid!"

"Easy now, big man," Marcus says. "I can be nice as the next guy, but only up to a certain point."

"You're the stupidest person in the world!"

"OK, I tried to warn you," Marcus says, reaching out and grabbing the boy by the collar. Twists the collar until the boy is on his knees again. "Your face looks so ugly right now," Marcus says. On the grill, the bank smolders and burns. "You should see it."

"You're a bully!"

"Hey now," Marcus says, twisting the collar tighter. "Those words hurt my feelings."

And Marcus would twist the collar again if the boy's mother didn't materialize at the sliding glass doors, Cliff in tow. The mother screams like the boy has never heard her scream, tells them to knock it off this instant. Wants to know what the hell is going on here?

"Marcus took the bank," the boy says, and then does something that will make it impossible to remember this moment with anything other than humiliation: he bursts into tears again and buries his face in his hands.

"Close that grill!" the mother says.

But Cliff has already stepped from behind her and closed the lid.

Marcus says it was all the boy's fault.

Cliff tells him to go inside. Now.

And what is the mother to make of this scene, her son and Marcus locked into some kind of adolescent combat, while her husband's old coin bank, that banal and detestable thing, inexplicably smolders on a grill that had, as far as she can recall, only held burgers and hot dogs? Smoke, thick and unnatural, rises from the grill's lid. The air feels heavy with lighter fluid. If ruin has a scent, this backyard reeks of it. See the smoke drifting into the neighbor's yard, as real and substantial as the boy's tears, which he wipes now, his breath heaving in his chest. This family has seen enough tears to last them for a good long while, but each day seems to show up with a fresh supply, unaware of surplus. Human misery, there's never a shortage of it. Surely, the neighbors will detect its odor, if they haven't already gotten too heavy a whiff this summer. This house where so much has gone up in smoke.

The mother puts her hand on the boy's shoulder, says, "Where's your sister?"

———

THE GIRL only has to try five more doors before finding Sarah's house, which is smaller than she recalls, and not nearly as close to the neighborhood entrance as her memory would have her mistakenly believe. But Sarah isn't the person who answers the door. The person who answers the door is Sarah's mother. She's wearing a robe, slippers, and sweatpants, her hair wrapped in a bath towel. Despite opening the door to find a ten-year-old girl on her doorstep for no likely good reason, Sarah's mother doesn't seem the least bit surprised to find her there, as if preadolescent girls showed up fairly regularly on her doorstep, trying, poorly, to explain who they were and why they were there. Difficult to explain really. The girl settles for "I'm a friend of Sarah's," to which Sarah's mother turns a look on her and says, flatly, "Sarah doesn't have any friends."

The girl tries, "Well, could you tell her I'm here?"

"I could," Sarah's mother says, "but I don't think it would help. My daughter is nobody's friend. She was always a lonely kid, and now she's an even lonelier adult. That's something you should know about her." The mother speaks like someone who has been interrupted either in the middle of taking an exam or administering it, the girl can't decide. A screen door divides the two of them:

Sarah's mother appears slightly shadowed behind it, her expression hard to read. "Please," the girl says. "I'd like to talk to her."

"There are three things you should know about my Sarah," Sarah's mother says, then holds up a hand to count them off. "One: Sarah is an excellent daughter. Two: Sarah is an excellent student. Three: Sarah is not an excellent friend."

"But," the girl says.

"I don't say that to criticize," the mother says, "I only say it to warn you."

"But could you please ask her anyway? Please?"

Sarah's mother sighs. "I'll do it, but I don't recommend it."

The girl says, "Can I come inside?"

But Sarah's mother has already disappeared inside the house, where the girl can now see a TV on a TV stand, a coffee table fitted out with books of crossword puzzles, newspapers, and a single glass ashtray overflowing with crushed cigarette butts. A sofa sags against the opposite wall, its shoulders wearing a blue-green afghan. An upright piano stands in the lee of a bookshelf, the piano topped with a creepy-looking doll strangely ensnared within a glass case. The girl can hear Sarah's mother calling out for Sarah, can hear Sarah say something back to her, but can't make out what the two of them are saying. A moment later, Sarah's mother appears at the screen door and says, "She says to tell you thanks for stopping by, but she's not available at the moment." Then, lower, "I tried to warn you."

"Please," the girl says, and feels herself beginning to cry. No, she will not cry. "Tell her I came here on my own. Please."

"Well," Sarah's mother says, "that is sort of impressive. Let me try again."

After a few more moments of conversation, occasional shouting, and a short wait followed by a longer one, Sarah appears at the screen door. She has her arms folded across her chest, her expression one of clear annoyance, the expression Sarah used to turn on the girl's father on those afternoons when he said he'd meet them later at the pool. Before the girl can say hello, Sarah says, "You shouldn't have come here."

"I just wanted to talk to you," the girl says.

"Mistake," Sarah says.

"Can I come inside?"

"Listen," Sarah says, sighs. "I know what you want to talk about, but there's really nothing to say. Whatever was between your dad and me is over now. That's all."

"But *why* is it over?" the girl says, louder than she intended. And damn it all if she doesn't start to cry, right there on Sarah's porch, like a baby. "Just tell me."

"That's what I'm trying to tell you. The why doesn't matter," Sarah says. "The why is just all the usual suspects: because things change. Because things end. Because people change."

"Because you changed," the girl says.

"Look," Sarah says. "I know this is hard for you."

"Don't talk to me like I'm a stupid kid!"

Sarah sighs. "I wasn't trying to talk to you like you're a stupid kid. You're not stupid."

"Then let me inside!"

"You're smart enough to be treated like an adult. And that's what adults do: they get over things, they move on, they don't wallow in the why."

"You're doing it again," the girl says. By now her hand is wet from all the tears she must wipe away. "You're talking to me like I'm dumb."

"I'm talking to you like I'd like someone to talk me, if I were in your shoes."

"But you aren't in my shoes. You have no idea about my shoes. You couldn't take two steps in my shoes."

"Look," Sarah says.

"Stop telling me to look!"

"I won't coddle you. If you want to be coddled, you came to the wrong place."

"What are you talking about?" the girl says, and damn it all if she doesn't let out a huge, childish, embarrassing sob. "I came here by myself just to see you. I hitched a ride."

"And now the ride is over, and I'm telling you to go home."

"Sarah!"

"This is all like a movie playing in your head," Sarah says. "The one where you're on a mission to find out the answer to things that have no answer. The one where you're the hero and I'm the bad guy."

"I didn't say you were the bad guy. Why are you acting like this?"

"The movie's over now. They're turning the lights on. Time to grab what's left of your popcorn and head to the exit."

"Sarah, please," the girl says. By this point, she must wipe both hands across her face, her stupid, childish face with all its stupid, childish tears. "I don't understand."

"You will," Sarah says, "one day."

"All I want is to talk to you, and you're treating me like this."

Sarah brushes her hair back, a stalling technique, the girl realizes; also, one meant to disguise the fact that Sarah has begun to cry too. "Go home," she says. "That's better than talking, trust me. Go home." And with that, Sarah steps away from the screen door, and leaves the girl wiping her hands across her face, her vision blurred enough that when Sarah's mother appears at the door again, at first the girl thinks it is Sarah, come back to tell her she's changed her mind, she can come in now, yes, they can talk.

"Well, now you know," Sarah's mother says. There's a weariness in the mother's voice the girl recognizes from back home, the voice her mother turns on her more and more often now, the one that greets her from the opposite side of the bathroom door, when the girl has been standing in front of the mirror as the mirror's fog loses its grip. The voice that subtly rejects the one in your head, a slight note of dissent, disapproval and exhaustion. Mother-daughter fatigue, it's spreading. Who can say where it will all end?

———

THE FATHER receives a phone call from his ex-wife. What she tells him before he can even register the oddity of receiving a phone call from his ex on a night when the children are at her house — at Mom's house, as the children say — is that their daughter has apparently run away. Left the house without anyone noticing. Gone for the past several hours. Before the father can ask who was watching them, or how it is possible for their daughter to slip away with no one noticing, another thought intrudes, so clear and unmistakable that he sets the others aside for now and shares the thought with his ex: the girl has probably gone to find Sarah. A name he's never spoken aloud to his ex. But there he is, saying it and knowing that he's right; he's sure of it. He tells his ex he'll call Sarah right now and then call her back once he's spoken with her. His ex says thanks, hangs up before the father realizes, not without guilt, that his daughter has given him a reason to get in touch with Sarah again. A thought he must chase away as he dials Sarah's number. Where is his daughter now? The father clears his throat, feels like a teenager calling a girl for the first time. Practices what he will say while the phone is still ringing. Hears Sarah answer and, for a moment, has no idea what he's about to say.

YOU WOULD THINK that a ten-year-old girl walking through a suburban neighborhood on a weeknight when most nearly everyone else is inside their homes, watching TV, and not in the least bit weeping into their halter top, would attract a certain degree of attention, but you would be wrong, the girl would have you know. The thing is, we're more invisible than we realize, prone to worrying about how others might see us, when, in fact, others hardly see us at all. It's true. These homes the girl is walking by might as well leave their shades open instead of closing them tight, for all anyone cares. No one is looking out; no one is looking in. What vanity to think otherwise. The girl has already made it to the neighborhood entrance without a single car stopping to ask if she's OK, and she guesses she should be thankful for that, but she can't help feeling the opposite too, this girl with one foot in adolescence and the other in wherever. Childhood. Well, forget all about that, each passing car would have her know; she should have listened to Gumma, it's over now. The world keeps wanting the girl to get the message, we're all on our own, but she's too thick to catch on. As bad as her brother really. She's ready to grasp the truth now, tonight, this girl is, even if her tears, those infantilizing things, have other ideas.

And, as if to prove that the girl has no idea about anything, the moment she leaves the neighborhood and starts walking along the two-lane road that leads, eventually, back to the gas station, the first pickup truck that passes by slows down, stops, and then reverses to where the girl stands, stops again. The girl fully expects it to be the bicycle perv or worse offering her a ride. But it isn't the bicycle perv, or at least not as far as the girl can tell. It's an older, grandfatherly type in a cowboy hat, plaid shirt, and the thickest pair of glasses the girl has ever seen. He's already got the passenger window down by the time the girl decides on her lie. Might as well add another to tonight's list.

"Excuse me, young lady," the man says, "but do you need a ride someplace?"

"No," the girl says, aims a fake smile his elderly way. "I'm just going for a little walk."

"A little walk? This is no place for a little walk. No, ma'am. I could barely see you until I was right up beside you. This is no place to be walking. Not safe."

The girl shrugs. "Well, my parents said it was OK."

The man says, "Well, I think I'd like a word with them. That's for sure."

In the distance, the girl can see another pair of headlights approaching from behind, knows that the man will either have to pull off to the shoulder to let the car pass or, more likely, just go along on his way. How easy this will all be, the girl thinks. How disappointing.

"They wouldn't want me talking to you," the girl says. "Stranger danger."

"Oh, I'm no danger," the man says. "I have two grandchildren your age. Married for fifty-three years. I've got a faith too. Do you have a faith?"

The girl considers this. Pictures the boys pretending not to look at her at the communion rail. "Not personally," she says.

"Then you are truly lost," the man says, but at that moment he must sense the headlights behind him, for he turns to look over his shoulder, then glances in the rearview mirror. "Hey," he says, apparently to the driver, "can't you see we're talking about our lord and savior, Jesus Christ?"

"Thanks for stopping by," the girl says.

The other driver honks at the man. "Honks at me," the man says.

"Bye," the girl says, but the man is already pulling away. The girl's first thought: wave at him as he leaves, to give the other car the impression, perhaps, that he has just dropped her off here on the side of the road. This is all legitimate, planned, deliberate. Nothing to see here. And the other car, as if to oblige the girl's scheme, passes by like she's not even there. Goodbye. The other car is off to wherever without so much as a thought about this girl standing on the side of the road, where ragweed waves dimly from behind a guardrail, bent in places, scraped in others. Beer cans, shorn of their pull-tabs, rest flatly beyond the rail's reach. The night air gives off a whiff of industrial-mowed grass. The girl is a part of the landscape really, this nonplace poorly lit by a cloud-veiled moon. This is no night for girls wandering along shadowy roads, searching for home. Drivers, keep your hands on the wheel; drive on.

———

AFTER CLIFF has banished Marcus to the guest bedroom, after the boy hears Cliff yelling in a way he has never heard Cliff yell before—didn't know he could really—and after the pain in the boy's arm has subsided to a low, throbbing ache, the boy remembers the bank. They left it on the grill, smoldering. It must still be out there, trapped within the grill's smoky darkness. Poor bank. The boy tiptoes past the guest bedroom, makes his way downstairs, opens the sliding glass doors to the deck.

The grill: closed, but still warm to the touch. The boy raises the lid and sees the bank lying there, blackened, ruined. The bank is still too hot to lift, but maybe with the grill tongs, which Cliff has added this summer, thoughtful Cliff. Problem: the bank is too heavy to lift, even with the tongs. Solution: use the tongs to drag the bank to the grill's edge, then catch bank with the serving tray Cliff uses for grilled corn on the cob, then carry serving tray to the picnic table to observe charred bank, which might be salvageable.

The damage could be superficial; he might be able to clean it away with some bathroom cleanser and rigorous scrubbing.

But when the boy prods the bank's door with the tongs, the door falls away. The door is a flimsy thing, nothing at all really. The boy sees the glossy coins within, dimes and nickels and quarters wearing a patina of lighter fluid, and it is like the coins are nothing the boy could ever want, ever. Dirty, worthless things. He leaves them there, to perish outside with the bank.

———

THE MOTHER knows this neighborhood well enough to know that if she travels the main drive and inspects every cul-de-sac that branches off from it, she will eventually find her daughter, provided, that is, that her daughter isn't hiding from her or worse, riding in a stranger's car—a possibility the mother cannot think about if she is to stay calm and keep focused, so she does not think about it. She tours the main drive twice, circles every cul-de-sac twice, says, "She's not here," to the benefit of her dashboard lights, brilliant this time of night, the sky outside an ultramarine-blue-leaning-black. This sky has a question for the mother: where would she go if she were the daughter? Where would she feel safe?

Of course.

Yes.

When the mother first sees her daughter in the headlights, walking along the shoulder, her gait as unmistakable as the jeans shorts and halter top combo the mother wishes she could tear from her body and swap out with overalls, the mother must remind herself not to yell at her. No. She must not scream at her daughter. She must not roll down the window and unleash all her anger and worry and fear on this girl, on whom so much has already been unleashed. This girl has seen her parents' lives split open. These past few months have either changed everything between them, the mother thinks, or the separation has left the family right where it found them, the mother cannot tell. Everything is as it was, in a way, and yet not at all, of course. The mother knows that; still, she could be convinced of either possibility. And as she slows the car to the shoulder and sees her daughter's rueful look of recognition in the headlights, the mother wants to ask her what she thinks. Whether they're someplace new or right where they've always been.

———

BUT HOW BAD could a single phone call be? When it is the phone call the father has just had with Sarah, with so many notes of finality sounding at once that it would perplex the most limber musician, the father can only think: bad. Very, very bad. That's what he would say, were anyone to ask him, but the father finds no comfort in the realization that no one ever will. Poor father, seeker of comfort, dreamer of consolation. See him at his bedside, telephone in his hand, its receiver offering up a generous helping of dial tone. It's time to end this sad little call; the father knows that. That's something the father is eminently aware of, yes. Still, the father hesitates. And he only sort of recognizes that he's been talking to himself for the past few minutes, fixing all the missteps he believes he made during the conversation, when, at last, he hangs up the phone and the room taunts him with silence.

———

AT FIRST, they do not speak. The girl climbs wordlessly into the passenger's seat without the mother's even having to roll down her window and say, "Hop in." She turns her body away from the mother, looks out the window at the whatever passing by. Not her best avoidance move, but it will do for now. A spare-tire technique the girl can ride for the next few minutes until she's safely home, her bedroom door primed for slamming. After a while, the mother tells her what happened, how she called her father and her father called Sarah and then called the mother back to confirm that the girl had been there tonight. Figures, the girl thinks; sold out by Sarah in the end. Why is nothing truly surprising anymore? The mother tells the girl she guessed she might head for the gas station. Looks over at the girl, but the girl's face is turned away. The mother keeps talking anyway. Realizes she's just talking to ease the ease-resistant tension between them, but what else can she do? Her daughter's face is so streaked with tears, the mother wants to ask her what happened with Sarah but knows she can't. Not now, at least, not tonight.

After a while, the girl says, "You didn't need to pick me up. I could have walked back by myself."

Careful, the mother thinks. Don't take the bait. Don't ask how she even got this far on her own. Surely someone gave her a ride, something the mother wants to ask about more than anything but settles for, "I thought you might need a lift."

"Well," the girl says, "you were wrong."

"You could have been abducted!" the mother says, and goddamn it all if she doesn't start to cry. "You could have been killed!"

The girl snorts. "Unlikely," she says.

Even though the mother realizes the girl has maneuvered her into a corner, she manages to find a corner within the corner when she says, "You are the most ungrateful daughter who ever lived."

"No," the girl says, "that would be you. Just ask Grandmom." Sometimes a killer move just presents itself to you, the girl thinks. Best bet is to grab on and see where it leads.

The mother says, "You have no idea what it was like to have a mother like Grandmom." Do not say, So I suggest you shut your ten-year-old mouth. "None whatsoever."

"Whatever," the girl says. "All I know is, when I get married, I'm going to stay married. No matter what." Sometimes it's like one killer move just yields to an even better one.

"Watch it," the mother warns.

"Only, I won't just do my own thing," the girl says, her advantage reaching the breaking point. "I won't be selfish. I'll think of others."

Hold, the mother thinks. Hold back.

"I'll put my family first," the girl says. "Unlike you."

And despite the mother's desire not to say what she's about to say, despite her so-called adult judgment, despite every opposition she can possibly think of—there are so many, too many to count at the moment—the mother finds herself saying, "The cat died."

"What?"

"The cat died," the mother repeats.

"How?" the girl says.

"Car," the mother says.

"No," the girl says, sobbing, her shoulders shaking. "No, that's not true." The girl tries to summon an image of the cat, but all that comes to mind is the time she stood at the top of the stairs and overheard her brother having a one-sided conversation with the cat, her dumb brother pouring milk into a bowl as he described a dream he'd had the night before in vivid and embarrassing detail. How excited her brother sounded, to have found a listener as interested in the dream as he was. The cat cannot be dead; that's something the girl needs to make her mother understand. The cat must be kept alive. If only the girl can tune her mother to that station, something good will have come out of tonight.

"Maybe it was a different cat," the girl says.

"No."

"But we hardly ever saw him anymore!" the girl cries. "You can't be sure."

The mother says she wishes she wasn't sure, but that's not the case. She tells the girl how she found the cat on the side of the road. How she tried to retrieve the body but couldn't bring herself to do it. How she had to ask Cliff to do it instead.

The girl weeps beside her, buries her face in her hands, says, "Why did you tell me that?" Imagines her brother pouring milk into a useless bowl, keeping his dumb dreams to himself. "I hate you for telling me that."

The mother says she didn't plan on it.

"Well, you did," the girl says, sobbing. "I wish you didn't. I'll never forgive you for telling me that. Never. Not in a million years."

A million years. The mother tries to think of that, fails. Says, "I'm sorry."

But the girl doesn't say anything. Hugs her knees to her chest, buries her head there. Why is the larger half of parenting failing to be a good parent? the mother wonders. Whose idea was that?

When the girl speaks next, it is in a voice the mother has only started to catch on to, the one the girl uses to subdue her brother without even making it seem like she's doing a thing. A voice of strange authority the mother isn't sure what to do with. The girl says, "We can't ever tell my brother."

The mother considers this. Finds the wisdom lurking there. "You're right," she says. "We can't ever tell him."

The girl imagines her brother gazing outside the sliding glass doors, where nothing appears, not even when he makes the little "psst-psst" sound that sometimes summoned the cat from thin air. "Ever," the girl says.

"Ever," the mother agrees, the distance between them momentarily narrowed, by a fraction of an inch, sure, but the mother can feel it nonetheless.

And the mother would reach out to her daughter — or say something perhaps — to contribute to the narrowing, but in the distance, she sees something she does not understand: the gas station, the one with the funny sign, is encircled by police cars, their lights blazing, furious, frenetic, a red-and-blue strobe that reaches across the intersection to where traffic has stopped, a line of cars ahead of them at this late hour, and, inexplicably, a row of diesel trucks blocking the intersection they must pass if they are to return home.

––––––

THAT NIGHT, the boy turns his fan to LOW. His hair, unwashed, mocks him with the smell of smoke.

––––––

THAT NIGHT, the father drinks bourbon and listens to music without anything vaguely resembling pleasure. He turns the music off, refills his glass.

––––––

LATER, the mother and the girl will understand what they saw that night. They will read about it in the newspaper and see it on the local news, again and again, what happened at the gas station. How an angry group of independent and commercial truckers, fed up with rising fuel costs, fearful that they wouldn't be able to afford to do their jobs anymore, began a protest that began innocently enough, with a few truckers holding signs, shouting slogans, and then quickly grew into something else, something darker, more menacing. One truck blocked the intersection and then another. More trucks joined the blockade. Locals, passersby, and others sympathetic to the protest, as the local news phrased it, joined them, relieved, at long last, to find a cause to hitch their collective anxiety to. Bars emptied. Friends called friends. The crowd grew. A full-on protest, fueled by booze, fear, and rage, soon took on the feel of a riot. Someone got the bright idea to drag a heap of an old car, left outside the station for repairs or abandoned for good, no one could really say, to the center of the intersection. And then someone else got the even brighter idea to light the car on fire.

And that's exactly what the mother and the girl see as they drive by: an old car of indeterminate year, make, and model, stunningly aglow in the middle of the intersection. Groups of men, beer bottles dangling from their hands, stand in the blaze's unappealing light. A few raise their fists, in defiance of something—what, the mother and the girl cannot say. Who are these men? What do they want? What are they doing here, on this summer night, standing before a burning car? Flames rise from the car's interior, the windows smashed, broken. The fire is so intense that several of the men have removed their shirts and tied them around their heads, lending the crowd a tribal aspect. A sense of ritual that's hard to place, one that's either on the side of community and fellowship or chaos and ruin. Hard to say. Are we all in this together or are we all apart from one another? Does our experience unite or divide us? The mother and the girl drive past the station, trying to decide. And it isn't until they arrive back home, where the mother and daughter take care to enter the house as quietly as they can, where the rest of the family is both awaiting and fearing their return, that it occurs to them that both are possible.

ACKNOWLEDGMENTS

Many thanks to Harry Stecopoulos for reading early drafts of this novel and helping to make it so much better and to Jim McCoy, Meredith Stabel, Allison T. Means, Carolyn Brown, and everyone at the University of Iowa Press for their editorial guidance and support. Thanks also to my students and colleagues at the College of Charleston. And many more thanks to my family, Malinda, Gus, and Ruby, for absolutely everything.

The Iowa Review Series in Fiction

Buddhism for Western Children
by Kirstin Allio

The Lines
by Anthony Varallo